THE ELFIN STONE

and other stories

Sarah Crabtree

Contents

THE ELFIN STONE

I thought it was you, Per.

As I stood on the corner of the familiar old street, clenching my mittened fingers against the Icelandic cold, I watched him approach. For one icy second, or maybe two, the blood stopped flowing. My heart turned into a strawberry lolly. There was something eerily magical in the thick white air. I had a flashback to that moment we shared: the moment our eyes locked, as we stood beside the Elfin stone.

Until now I never really believed the true power of the Elfin stone. In your country it is grouped with other natural landmarks named *álagablettir*, whispered to be elf-occupied and enchanted. I know your mother painstakingly explained the legend of the *Huldufólk*, or hidden people; how if you truly believe, you can press your ear against the rock and listen to the heart beating within. *Huldufólk* somewhat resemble humans, wear 17th-century clothing, farm sheep, pick berries and have been seen at Sunday church. At least I think she told me that. Alternatively, I read it in a newspaper.

In other parts of the world people see Madonnas weep and witness images of the living dead.

I am not worthy enough to disbelieve. I was so sure it was Per.

Huldufólk are more active in winter, your mother told me. They only come out of the rocks to search for food, or to tempt unwary travellers to their demise.

It was the movement of his feet along the crystallised pavement: that purposeful leaning towards the right as if negotiating an incline. A rush of adrenalin forced audible beats out of my frozen heart. In the silence of the twilit town I wondered if he would hear them. As he drew closer I smiled, and of course the moment was shattered by a stranger's scornful glance and by my own devastation.

It was an easy mistake, and yet still foolish.

In this sparsely-populated wilderness there are perhaps many men who share those characteristics, your characteristics, so evident despite the inevitable layers of clothing against the stinging cold. Like you he carried an easy height of six foot one or two, so starkly contrasted to my shrew-like stature. Though the short hours of daylight denied me the knowledge of the colour of his hair and eyes, I knew he shared your Nordic colouring. I wonder if he guessed I am Celtic-skinned, black-haired and brown-eyed.

I wonder if he cared.

With the devastation of disappointment came the pain of my supposed unattractiveness. History was not about to give me a second chance. I tried to console myself with suppositions such as he might already be involved, or pre-occupied, or gay.

Perhaps he was grieving.

I paused to listen to his footsteps, ice-crunching, heavy and solid. He was rounding the corner now, past the Elfin stone.

I wanted to call out your name. Just in case.

The *Huldufólk* invade farmhouses at Yuletide. They cannot be avoided. Even the roads are built around their rocky homes.

At home in England, we have Roman roads that are so straight.

"Huldufólk"

The letters froze like solid glass tumblers, like the icicles chiselled on to the pastel-painted ledges of the cosy homesteads of this Frozen Eden.

I remember your reaction when I first called your homeland Frozen Eden. You replied, "Then you haven't found Heaven here with me?"

I laughed and asserted, "Heaven is for angels, Per."

For once or twice afterwards if I were to describe a meal prepared by your mother, a drinking evening with your friends, and a kiss beside a waterfall of icicles beneath a werewolf moon as 'Heaven', you would gently reprimand me with my own words: "Heaven is for angels."

I remember the night of the anniversary of your grandfather's death when your mother would gather together as many as were willing to trek out of their homes, to tell once more of the legend that took her to Greenland and back again home to Iceland. First, she would serve us all with Greenlandic coffee, a warming tradition of coffee with whiskey, Kahlúa and whipped cream, topped by Grand Marnier that she had set on fire first. Then the legend of how her family, father, mother, brother and she herself made the treacherous voyage to Greenland on her father's whim. He took out a loan and bought a fishing boat. The short Arctic summer was still in full blaze when they left, but before they were within sight of the harbour, winter arrived early.

As evening turned into the blackness of night, the air around the boat began to freeze. Icy waves lashed against the weakening craft. Above even the sky seemed frozen, as if they were already beneath the ocean and the sky above was its chilled surface, like an ice rink. In the midst of this terror, grandfather slipped and fell into the treacherous water. Mother tried to pull him out, but brother and sister intervened lest both should be lost. They knew the lighthouse keeper would already have alerted the emergency services. Indeed the children saw silhouettes of the helicopters against the frosted sky. Too late to save grandfather, whose petrified body washed up on the shore they had so nearly reached in safety, as it turned out.

Only grandmother settled in Greenland. Each night she would wake fancying she heard her husband yelling for her on the Arctic tundra, as his soul reached for hers. A piercing cry, followed swiftly by a lower-toned "No!" It would repeat six or seven times, maybe even a dozen, and then disappear into the night.

If one were a deep sleeper then one might think it were part of a dream. Somebody woken from alcoholic slumber might even think some-one was being murdered out there.

If one were a naturalist, then one might decide it was a vixen call-ing to her mate, who barks in response. Arctic foxes howling under a winter moon.

Whatever the real reason was, grandmother stayed and died in Greenland. Brother and sister each returned to Iceland to study. Brother now, too, had passed to that Frozen Eden beyond. This was truly the sister's legend to share until it became the legend of her son and so forth into eternity.

The stranger might well have been able to tell me the road and number of your mother's house. They say it is almost impossible to meet a local who cannot put you in touch with another local. England was like that once. I retraced my steps on second thoughts. But the stranger had entered the yellow-lit bar at the end of the adjoining street. He must have done, because there was no sign of him anywhere. Only the Elfin stone loomed, willing me to move towards it.

Yet my confidence was falling away from me. The stomach- churn-ing anticipation I had felt that very morning, when my alarm woke me at 6.15 for the taxi to the airport, swapped places with doubt. Self-doubt. The worst kind. Three years ago I fell in love.

Now I am falling.

It sounds so corny: on the same lines as one of those (hopefully) eye-catching sub-titles that will clinch the sale of yet another magazine.

But who's buying now? I am twenty-eight, look thirty-six. Somebody told me twenty-eight is over-the-hill in New York. So what about thirty-six? And in this cream-dream landscape, what's the cut-off date? Does the shortness of the summers allow a little leeway?

We are always asking ourselves questions; and when someone is brave enough to speak or publish an answer, we tear them apart. We question their nerve, their audacity. "Their downright cheek." That's what my mother would say.

The cold was fingering its way through my blue woollen gloves and tormenting my toes through my black suede boots. I had paused for too long. How foolish an act for a woman who had lived in this country for four seasons and who should know the rules of survival. In a land cold enough to freeze a husky's tongue to a water barrel, I should have known better than to stand alone on this Arctic street.

But I was not alone. My eyes bored into the Elfin stone. The Friday night revellers were now taking to the streets: healthy young people in bright warm clothing, excitedly greeting each other, planning their parties, anticipating their love affairs. One or two of them smiled at me. They were trying to be friendly. Or maybe they thought they recognised me.

How could they, almost two years after my disappearance?

Frantically I scanned the hordes of young people aiming in my direction. But it was impossible to check each face in the grey and orange light. And after all I am not sure I really did want anyone to recognise me. There was always the chance that had I seen you, you would have been with someone else; another girl, someone more of your own kind, tall and blonde and blue-eyed, with the face of an angel

I see the image of this many times. Occasionally I dream it, often I force it into my mind. Then usually when I have eaten something healthy like marinated herrings, gravadlax, with rye bread - you see I have taken to your country's gourmandise - I console myself with a full stomach and a recollection of our words: "Heaven is for angels."

I miss my friends, your friends, our friends. London is lively, but lonely. I miss the blue and amber candlelit suppers. I miss our shelter from the cold. I even miss that sulphur smell. When I first visited this country, it made me feel sick. When I returned to England to the smell of taxi-cabs and double-deckers, I felt homesick. Yet England is the country of my birth. Except for that little drop of Welsh blood - hence the Celtic skin - I am pretty well pure English.

After I watched the revellers disappear round the Elfin stone, I dithered. The Celtic part of me followed them. I always said that was my adventurous side. But my English body rooted to the icy pavement. It was time to move on. But in a different direction. I returned to my overnight room and slept a dreamless sleep. To sleep without dreaming is so unusual for me. You see, almost every night since I left Iceland two years ago, I have dreamed about you standing beside the Elfin stone. That's why I had to return. Don't you see? I couldn't leave things open-ended. I had to make sure you really didn't want me anymore. Everything points to the Elfin stone. And everything comes from it, too.

I have faith now. Another souvenir to take home with me. Thank you.

When I woke I only had twelve more hours left in your country, which once was mine also. I decided, and as my own mother would have put it "for old time's sake" to make an excursion to a place we used to haunt...

...when both of us were in love.

It was ten o'clock in the morning, still dark and the temperature, of course, was well below zero. I am told that London is the warmest city in Great Britain. That is why all the box and bag people head for it. But

I believe I am correct in saying the warmth is caused by its pollution.

Mount Hekla looked bad-tempered that day. She seemed to scowl at me in the same way as the Viking stranger who refused to acknowledge me.

I could take a hint. I knew when it was all over. Your coldness towards me and the way you no longer looked at me, I mean really looked at me, meant there was no need for words. But then you were never loquacious, and I was never silent. I think that is why I became a writer, so I could pen all my opinions instead of boring you with them.

I gave Mount Hekla a final nod of respect. A shudder went through my body: I remember you told me once the Vikings thought of that mountain as the gateway to Hell...

The words 'I love you' are stored out there somewhere, frozen forever; imprisoned within the Elfin stone.

It was time to return to Reykjavik. I had decided to catch the earlier plane back to London. I did not want to be away from my daughter for too long; and my career is paved with deadlines. But then you know that already: about the deadlines, I mean...

"Andrea! Andrea!"

I think that old Elfin stone must have been playing tricks on me again. For I swore I could hear somebody calling my name. I turned, but apart from the other busy commuters, anxious to catch their plane, nobody seemed to be approaching.

I entered the airport terminal, double-checking I had remembered my passport and ensuring my wallet was safely ensconced in my shoulder bag. I have always been a little paranoid about the safe-keeping of my valuables since my purse was stolen in Paris.

"A-a-ndrea! A-a-ndrea!" I heard the voice again.

Here I am, almost ready to leave. Everything appears in order. My suitcase is, of course, bulkier than when I arrived. As well as the ubiquitous supermarket carrier of soiled linen, there is also enclosed a child-size sweatshirt of Mount Hekla I was unable to resist, (it should fit her in a year or so), and one or two little souvenirs for my London colleagues. Perhaps I will keep that paperweight encasing the tiny fake Elfin stone, just to remind me...

"A-a-a-ndrea! A-a-a-ndrea!"

You see, I never took back any souvenirs the last time. It was a different parting then. This time it is for good. I have laid all my old ghosts to rest in that desert landscape, and any other uncertainties have been swept away by the Arctic breezes as they skim off the powder snow.

"A-a-a-a-ndrea! A-a-a-a-ndrea!"

It's too late to turn back now. I have said my last goodbyes. I travel a great deal with my work, taking my daughter with me on lengthier trips when I can. Klaus, my new partner, is very good, though. He treats Kim as if she were his.

"Andrea!"

I still find airports heartbreaking. There is something so final when those wheels leave the ground: a car can always perform a U-turn, a train stops at the next station, even a boat can drop anchor...like a stone...

...but a plane taking off says goodbye...forever...I can almost hear it in the scream of the engines.

"Andrea!"

And then no more as we cruise, settled back with our duty frees. My mother said it is always hardest for those left behind. That reminds me, I must give her a call when I get back. There is so much to catch up on. My, this gin and tonic tastes good.

* * *

A lonely figure returns to a darkening street. The supernatural shadows of the Arctic swallow up his silhouette, merging it with the Elfin stone. London is far away with its bright lights and shimmering river.

It serves you right, Per. You had your chance, back there beside the Elfin stone.

I knew that was you.

IN TO WIN

"A-ar-a-r-gh!" A piercing scream came from the living room.

"Whatever are you two getting up to?" Dom tore himself away from the kitchen sink to check out the damage.

"Don't worry, Dad," said eleven-year-old Charlotte. "I've only beaten Paul at Monopoly."

"It sounded like you were killing him."

Paul cried, "It's not fair. She got all the money and all the best hotels."

"Sounds like a typical woman to me," muttered Dom under his breath.

"What was that, Dad?" Paul looked at him puzzled.

"Oh, nothing, lad." He ruffled the eight-year-old's short blonde hair. "It's pizza for tea. Your favourite."

"Great, Dad!" Paul seemed to have forgotten his disappointment. The groans in his stomach spoke louder than words.

"Are you going to help me clear up this game?" came Charlotte's bossy tones. "Or is it going to be left to me to tidy up as usual?" Tidy was emphasised too loudly.

"Go on, Paul." Dom grinned. "Do as the lady says. Otherwise there'll be no peace for the rest of the evening." He went back to his pizza preparation, comprising all of opening a cardboard box, removing a plastic wrapping and a sliding of the food item into a pre-heated oven, along with frozen chips.

"Just stop it, will you?" came a shout from the living room.

"You're a cheater!" "Am not!"

"Are!" "Am not!"

"All right! That's enough!" Dom stood in the doorway, arms akimbo. "There am I slaving away over a hot stove, and all you two can do is argue over a stupid game!"

"It's all her fault!" yelled Paul. "She didn't add up her money properly. I almost won." Tears streamed down his face. "I almost won!" he sobbed.

"But you didn't!" shouted Charlotte. "I won fair and square. And I didn't cheat! No way!"

The front door slammed. "Hello, you lot!" Sand was home. Dom turned to her and pecked her on the cheek. "Hi, Sand. Oh great, you got the side salad."

Sand wrinkled up her nose. "I can smell something burning." Dom dashed into the kitchen just in time to rescue the oven glove from burning to a crisp on the hob.

"Never mind." Mum grinned. "I've got a surprise for everyone!"

"What's that, Mum?" Charlotte was coming up just behind her.

"A lady I work with has given me a family ticket for tenpin bowling. She won it in a charity draw. Said we could have it."

"That was nice of her," said Dom. "When shall we go?"

"This evening after tea too soon?" asked Sand as she tugged open the cutlery drawer.

"Yes, please, Mum!" chorused the kids.

An hour and a half later they arrived at the bowling alley. Dom was even more excited than Paul and Charlotte when he saw the bright lights. And he was very impressed with the high-tech score board.

"It was nothing like this when my dad used to take me!"

"Well things were a bit backward in the fifties, weren't they Dad?" said Charlotte importantly.

"Seventies, you cheeky madam!" corrected Dom. "I'm not that old."

He checked over the different sized bowling-balls available. "Some of these are too light for me," he advised. "But they'll be just right for you three."

"I thought you said you hadn't played since the seventies!" Sand said indignantly. She selected a middle-weight bowling-ball and scored a strike.

"Awesome, Mum!" screeched the kids in unison.

"Okay, we'll just have a practice run first," said Dom.

"You mean that doesn't count?" Sand glared at him.

"Come on, Sand! We've got to give the kids a chance." He rolled his bowling-ball like a true pro.

As Sand watched Dom's bowling-ball go in for the kill, she said, "Somebody's got to win." The ball struck home. "And if you carry on playing like that it won't be you, love."

"Oh, Dad," bleated Charlotte. "You only knocked one down."

"That's all right, sweetheart." He chuckled. "Remember I said the first go was just a practice run?"

After they'd each had a practice, Dom said, "Right. Now we're going to be playing for real. Just do your best. Enjoy it! It's only a game remember?"

"But I really want to win, Dad!" pleaded Paul.

"Paul!" reprimanded Sand. "Do you honestly expect us to play badly just so that you can win?"

"Well Dad's managing very well!" piped up Charlotte as she watched Dom's bowling-ball miss every single pin on his next go.

"Hard luck, love." Sand patted Dom on the back kindly. "Better luck next time!" She selected her ball and got another strike.

"Sand!" hissed Dom out of the kids' earshot. "You're playing too well."

"Rubbish!" she hissed back. "I'm only a few points in front of Paul at the moment."

"Strike!" yelled Paul. "I got a strike! My first strike!" He threw his arms up in the air and cheered. Even Charlotte forgot their rivalry for a few seconds and stared fascinated at the animated scoreboard which produced a jolly little green man with a great grin.

Soon it was Dom's turn again. He decided on a change in tactics. He selected a slightly lighter ball. This time he managed to knock down two pins.

At the end of the game session, Paul won and Charlotte and Mum came equal second. Dad was very quiet as they made their way back to the car.

"Are you okay, Dad?" said Charlotte, as Dad started the engine.

"Is it because he lost?" whispered Paul.

"Okay, I'll come clean." Dom chuckled. "Though I try hard not to let it show—"

"You're ever so slightly a bit of a—" Sand interrupted, and they mouthed at each other: "Bad loser."

Sand pecked him affectionately on the cheek before plugging in her seatbelt. "And we thought you were letting us win," she teased. "How about a game of Monopoly before bed?"

"No thank you!" chorused the others.

IN THE SWIM

"It's your turn to take Vikki swimming today," said James, snatching up the newspaper and burying his head in it.

"Okay, that's fine. Just fine." Kelly banged her coffee mug down on the table. "You know how much I hate that chlorinated water and my swimming costume's shrunk because it's got wet too much-"

"Ha!" He interrupted her. "Shrunk? Don't be daft, Kel. You just need to cut down on all those homemade pastries you've been stuffing yourself on."

"And what about you and those cocktails with whipped cream. Take a look at your own waistline, why don't you." Kelly looked down and spotted a very forlorn-looking Vikki, standing there in her little yellow bikini, clutching her red swimming ring. "Oh, sweetie," she said. "I'm sorry. This is supposed to be our annual summer holiday and Mummy and Daddy are arguing even more than when we're at home."

"So will you take me swimming, Mummy?" Vikki looked up at her with big brown eyes. "I can almost swim a length now."

Vikki sighed and said, "Of course, sweetie. Just give Mummy a bit of time to get her swim-gear ready. Daddy's far too busy to take you this morning." Kelly glared over her shoulder at James, who buried his face even more deeply into the paper.

Half an hour later, she and Vikki were approaching the pool. There was a water aerobics class being held. So they sat quietly at the side until it was finished. The rep taking the class, stopped the music, packed up the CD player, and then had a friendly word with the lifeguard on duty.

It was another beautiful day in the Spanish resort. Kelly splashed plenty of sunblock over Vikki and herself, and then slid carefully into the shallow end of the pool. Vikki jumped in, splashing a couple of older women, who looked a bit disgruntled at getting their designer bathing suits wet. Kelly pretended not to notice. It was, after all, a swimming pool, and you were supposed to get wet in a pool.

"Mummy!" called Vikki. "Why don't you come and swim down in the deep end with me?"

"Not today, darling. I'm enjoying it here." A big boy in blue trunks kerplunked into the water almost washing her over to the other side. "Lovely," she said, forcing a smile.

Vikki splashed around a bit more in the deeper end. By now the shallow end was getting pretty packed with more and more non- swimmers of all ages and sizes.

"Mummy!" called Vikki more impatiently this time. "You're being silly staying down there. Come and swim over here with me."

"No really." Kelly grimaced. "It's fabulous here." Another even bigger boy threw himself towards the pool, missed by a mile and knocked her flying. She went face-first into the water, and came up spluttering. When she'd finally recovered, she noted the two fashion-conscious women had abandoned the pool and headed for the beach bar. They were drinking cocktails… and yes, James was over there drinking a cocktail, too. He saw Kelly looking, and waved across, then affected a swimming motion at her, coaxing her into leaving the safety of the shallows and head for the open peril of the deep end.

When a beachball smacked into her face, that decided it for her. She would take her chance and swim.

So she did. It wasn't a very graceful swimming motion. More doggy than crawl, and as she pushed and panted towards the deeper end, she suddenly felt her nerve go. When she couldn't touch the bottom with her toes, she launched herself upwards with supernatural strength and flung herself towards where Vikki was waiting for her at the other end of the pool.

Somehow she made it, and grabbed hold of the side, panting.

"Mummy! Mummy! That was wonderful. You are such a great swimmer!" screamed Vikki.

"Help!" said Kelly. "Get help! This is the first time I've ever swum in the deep end and I don't think I have the strength to get out on my own."

Luckily the lifeguard had spotted she'd lost her breath and he dived in to assist her. He soon had her out on the side on her back and was about to administer artificial respiration, when James appeared, followed by the two designer costume women.

"I don't think that's necessary, thank you." He waved away the lifeguard, and helped Kelly up. "Why do you have to make such an exhibition of yourself?"

Before Kelly replied, Vikki piped up: "But, Daddy. You NEVER swim with me in the deep end either!"

"Right, dear," said one of the designer swimsuit ladies, sounding a lot jollier after her mid-morning cocktail. "I think it's time Jeanie here and I rectified that. Come along!"

"Right you are, Hazel," said Jeanie, sounding a lot jollier, too. And they each grabbed one of James's arms and hit the water.

"Aaaargh!" said James, his legs and arms floundering. "Help me!"

"Oh dear," said Jeanie. "Better rescue him!" Between them they managed to yank him out. The lifeguard blew his whistle and joined in the rescue.

Everybody else by the pool gave them all a round of applause. Later, when Vikki, Kelly and James had got dried off, James said sheepishly, "Shall we do something a little less wet, like go for a walk on the beach tomorrow?"

"Yes, please!" said Vikki, grinning from ear to ear. So they did.

And it rained!

SCARLET RIBBONS

Once there was a remarkable young lady named Delia.

She had curly, golden-brown hair and enormous blue eyes just like a real fairytale princess; except she wasn't really a princess and hadn't met the handsome prince.

The nearest she'd come to meeting this mythical character was when she bumped into a nervous, yet rather dishy young man named Carl. 'Bumped' was literally what had happened, as their supermarket trolleys had collided when he was trying to avoid the pyramid of baked bean cans and she was performing a U-turn after spotting her favourite pasta shapes were on special offer.

Although Delia was sure Carl knew he'd met the woman of his dreams, his silver lady, the person he wanted to share the rest of his shopping days with, Delia was not so certain of her own feelings. While she accepted she was in love with Carl as much as she thought it was possible to be in love with a man - especially one who wasn't actually a handsome prince - she felt (arguably) that there had to be more to life than just meeting a nice chap, marrying, having his kids and subsequently doing all his shopping.

"I do love him," she said to her younger sister, Sally during their monthly get-together in the restaurant on the top floor of the smartest store in town. "It's just that I want to do something with my life before I actually get married, live in suburbia and all that sort of thing."

Sally, who was almost as pretty as her sister, was rummaging through her handbag. "Ah," she said. "There it is." She extracted a small paper bag. "Now then." She looked her sister squarely in the eyes. "Has he actually asked you to marry him?"

A furrow marred the older girl's lovely strawberries-and-cream brow. "Well, not in so many words," she answered. "Though he has dropped a few hints."

Sally leaned towards her sister. "Has he got down on bended knee and said 'Delia, will you be my wife?'"

She fidgeted a little uncomfortably. "Well, no, he hasn't. But that's not the point."

"Not the point?" Sally raised her voice. "I think it's the whole point and nothing but the point."

"Don't be silly, Sally." Delia's exquisite Cupid's bow formed a perfect pout, rather as if she were about to blow a kiss at the young waiter who was approaching them with the prawn cocktails.

"Don't be a fool to yourself, Sis." The younger girl nodded a thanks to the waiter and then removed something from the little paper bag. "Be honest. You want the man to propose and he hasn't."

"No, I don't. And why are you putting those silly ribbons in your hair?" She dug her spoon into the cocktail dish. "You look like a schoolgirl."

"That's because I am, silly." Sally flicked back her blonde plaits. "After I've lunched with you I've got my school farewell dance to attend. It's an Austrian theme and I've got a sweet costume. I found these ribbons in the remnants bin downstairs. Do they remind you of something?"

"No." Delia sulked through her prawns.

"Come on!" the schoolgirl coaxed.

Delia swallowed a mouthful then answered, "Well, you're obviously dying to tell me."

Her sister beamed triumphantly. "That song you used to love when we were little. The one Jim Reeves sang. 'Scarlet Ribbons'. Remember?" Satisfied, she began eating her own prawns.

Delia stopped chasing the final prawn round the dish. "Oh, yes. Gosh. That takes me back."

Encouraged, Sally added "It was about a little girl who desperately wanted some scarlet ribbons and her daddy went out in the night to try to get her some..."

The older girl took up the story: "But all the shops were closed." Tears like little diamonds formed in the corners of her eyes. "And the next morning when she awoke there were...

"Lovely ribbons, scarlet ribbons!" they both sang out.

The young waiter cleared his throat. "Excuse me. Has Madam finished with her dish?"

Delia looked at the sad little prawn she had failed to catch and sighed "Yes, thank you. You may take it away."

"Delia?"

"Yes, Sally."

"Take my sisterly advice. Don't let that fish swim away."

Our fairytale heroine was bewildered. She returned to her studio flat and sat on her narrow little bed, thinking very hard. That night was to be a long one. She slept badly. In her tortured dreams she saw Carl kissing strange, beautiful women.

The next morning (a Saturday) she paid particular attention to her make-up. At ten o'clock the telephone rang.

"Hi! It's Carl. Look, about dinner at eight..." He sounded hesitant.

"Yes?" Her heart was thumping.

"Um, I'd like to do something different. Just for a change."

Something special, she thought. Something romantic. Oh, am I really ready for this?

"Yes." He paused for a moment. Then added "I'd rather not go out tonight at all. Can we call it off? It's just that I'm busy today and well, you know how things are." His voice trailed off ominously.

Know how things are? Of course she knew how things were. He was trying to let her down gently. He was trying to tell her he'd found somebody else. She'd played the elusive butterfly for too long and...she replaced the receiver and bawled like a colicky baby all over her lurid pink duvet.

Ten minutes later she stopped crying and sat up. She felt a little better for getting all that out of her system. She'd soon forget him. There were plenty more fish swimming around. She'd find somebody else.

Delia looked at herself in the dressing-table mirror: her hair was sticking up, her mascara made her look like a panda, and her lipstick had bled all round her mouth. She was looking into the eyes of a clown. Then she eyed the little Pierrot doll sitting on the shelf above her bed. They didn't let him into Heaven because he broke his promise and played with the children. What a stupid story that was. Like the one about the scarlet ribbons. This fairytale stuff was all stupid. Even so, she had another good bawl over the lurid pink duvet; and when she gazed in the mirror again she looked even more clown-like than the poor old Pierrot.

I'm not going to chase after him. I've never chased after a man in my life, and I'm not going to start now, she said to herself as she exited her flat without a jacket and wearing only a thin pink nylon blouse and grey linen skirt. Shivering slightly, she unlocked the door of her blue Mini.

He's not even very good looking, she decided as her key found its way into the ignition. Okay, he's got nice brown eyes. She drove off.

His dark hair curls rather nicely over his forehead, rather like that fellow in that Jane Austen novel. She stopped at the traffic lights. He's a bit skinny, but he's got nice legs and very attractive arms.

That last thought did it: the very idea of never ever falling into Carl's loving arms again was rather hard for Delia to handle. She slumped over the steering wheel and sobbed in accompaniment to the depressed horn.

Delia was still very young, and you'd have to be pretty hard-hearted not to excuse her for holding up a long lane of traffic while she hogged the middle of the road on a green light.

"Oi, Miss!" A large, bald, tattooed gentleman tapped on her side window. She wound it down without bothering to look up at him. He shouted, "I ain't one for road rage. Not me. Too much of a gent. But can't you see the light's green?"

When the tear-stained panda doll stared up at him he backed away in horror. "Sorry." The clown-mouth smiled. "I won't hold you up any longer." She jammed her foot on the accelerator and left him standing there in a cloud of exhaust fumes.

Five minutes later Delia was parked outside the blue door of Carl's Victorian apartment. She took a deep breath, and checking her appearance in the rear-view mirror, she snatched up a travel tissue to repair the cosmetic damage. Smoothing out the creases in her skirt and blouse, she proceeded to climb the three steps and rapped the brass door knocker.

The door swung open. "Why, Delia. Come in!"

How could Carl be so casual about all this? Their relationship was over, her heart was in pieces, and he was looking so cool about the whole thing.

"Sit down," he offered. "Can I get you a drink?"

"No, thank you. I won't be staying long." Not knowing what to do with her arms, she decided to fold them across her chest.

"In a hurry, are you?" He smiled. Standing there in smartly-pressed jeans and wearing the royal blue pullover she'd given him last Christmas, he looked so good that she couldn't bear to look at him.

"Yes, I am in a hurry," she stuttered. "Actually I'd better leave now." She unfolded her arms.

"But you've only just got here," he protested.

"So I have." Delia folded her arms again. She felt like an actress who has forgotten her cue.

"Darling?" Carl moved towards her.

"Right then." She stepped back and raised her eyes to the ceiling.

"Will you marry me?"

"What?" Her arms fell to her side. She hadn't quite grasped what he'd said. She was more interested in two strands of something reddish hanging from the mock-chandelier. "What was that you said?" She stumbled out the words, her eyes still fixed on the scarlet ribbons above. Scarlet ribbons that made a girl's dream come true. "Why? The interfering little-"

"I said 'Will you marry me?'"

As in all happy endings the princess, who in this case is not a real princess, falls into the arms of the handsome prince, who in this case isn't really all that handsome and is definitely not a real prince.

Our pretend princess thinks about the little sister who interfered so romantically. And the most important part of the story is that Delia said "Yes!"

OVER THE RAINBOW

"Come back to the city!" I pleaded again with my elder sister Claire.

She wouldn't listen. But then how many older sisters take the advice of a younger one? Exactly. Only now I felt it was my turn to keep an eye on her. Like lots of people, every now and then I wonder where all those years have gone. It only seems like yesterday when Nanna Rose used to laugh kindly at us when Claire and I packed our little picnic baskets and she would call after us: "You two off to seek your fortunes?!" I am sure there was more that followed. One of us probably got stung by a bee, or we dropped our jam sandwiches, or maybe I fell over and grazed my knee. I only remember the really good bits: the long summer sunny holidays, playing on the beach near Nanna's home, and then the excitement of moving to the city when Daddy changed jobs. I happily became a city girl, but Claire moved to the country with her husband Joel and her potter's wheel.

Then sadly three months after settling into their new home, Joel died suddenly.

Again, I tried to coax Claire back to the city.

Instead, she persuaded me to stay in the country with her for a week. "I'll have you converted from town to country mouse." She laughed, and for a moment I think we forgot how hard those past six months had been for her. Deep down, I wondered how she would cope when the summer ended and the dark nights drew in. I knew if she budgeted carefully, she could manage to afford to stay in her cottage. It just worried me that she had barely had chance to make new friends before tragedy hit her. Her nearest neighbours were busy farmers. I had a two bedroom flat in the city and she knew that she was more than welcome to come and live with me.

On the last afternoon of my stay, Claire pulled down both our coats from the hook by the front door, and said, "Jenny, let's go and seek our fortunes!"

It was already dusk, and I missed the streetlights of the city. I was about to grab a torch, when Claire said, "You don't need that when we have the stars."

She was right. As usual. It was to be a beautiful starry night. I forgot that you don't get to see the stars in the bright lights of the city. Earlier, Claire said, there had been a rainbow. I missed that too. Either it was because I was looking out the wrong window, or perhaps I needed to change my glasses. I wouldn't say the week together had been fraught. It was more that she and I had very different ideas. Going for a walk in fading light down a muddy path and treading in heaven knows what wasn't my first choice of spending my last night in the country. But tomorrow I would be back in my beloved city in my tidy flat. May as well make the most of the fresh country air (and its farmyard smells!) while I had the chance.

And that's when we heard it. I have never been so frightened in all of my life.

The only way I can describe the noise is by saying it sounded like a beast that was either very angry or very hungry. It was a low rumble that grew into a bellow like something from another world. I have never been so keen to get out of the country as I was that evening.

"Jenny!" My sister was saying my name over and over. I had started to run away, tripped and almost fell into a muddy puddle. Again she was calling my name, and saying, "You're running the wrong way. We need to get the farmer. One of his sheep has got his horns stuck in a hedge. He's jammed tight, poor thing."

Right again. Claire persuaded me to talk nicely to the ram using soothing words to calm him (and yours truly!) down, while she bolted off to the farm, which was in the opposite direction. Soon she was back with the farmer named Miles and his son Nick.

"Silly fool shouldn't be here," Miles grunted.

Claire whispered, "Don't worry. He doesn't mean you." I nudged her, trying not to laugh. I was worried the sheep was hurt. But it all turned out well. Phil the ram had had a busy day and then run off to seek his fortune elsewhere. It took a bit of digging and turning over of the earth and cutting back of the hedge, but Phil was released.

And that's when I spotted the pot of gold.

* * *

Six months later, I'm sitting in Claire's recently redecorated and cosy lounge, sipping a cup of strong coffee. The doorbell just rang, and she has gone to answer it. It's probably either Miles or his lovely wife Lucy dropping in. Their son Nick will be back working in IT in the city. The same city I will be returning to later on in the week.

Remember that pot of gold I spotted? It was an old clay one circa 1960s, filled with buttons and a few worthless old coins. But Claire has been busy with her potter's wheel and making her rainbow pots. (It was a special glazing process she learned from a video on the internet.)

"We aren't completely in the Dark Ages up here," she joked. "Even in the middle of winter!" She gets to sell her pots in Miles' and Lucy's farm store to "those fancy folks who come up from the city."

She couldn't possibly be referring to me, I decide, as I take down our coats from the hook by the door. It's a beautiful starry night. When it's just Claire and me again, I'm going to suggest we go out and seek our fortunes. One more time. For old time's sake!

THE LITTLE SHOP ON THE CORNER OF THE STREET

"Sandy," said Bill. "We can't afford it. We did the maths. It's too much of a risk. I'm sorry, love."

That was last week. Although Bill had said the same thing several times over, as Sandy tried to remonstrate with him. She knew that he was right on paper. They had asked several banks if they would be willing to lend the couple the money to take over the grocery business. The answers were pretty much of a muchness. Most were only willing to lend money at extortionate interest rates. Others wanted the couple's house as security. Still more just shook their collective heads.

"The retail industry is dead in the water," said one bank manager.

"How could your little grocery store compete with the corporations? Thirty, twenty, even ten years ago I might have been able to be more optimistic. It's all internet business now."

Even as Sandy mulled over all of this, an online delivery van drove past and pulled up outside the house three doors from her.

And then she was transported to her grandparents' house, "The Store". She was four years old again.

There was the living room, a step back into the 1930s with its faded black and white photographs on the wall, the small red elephant with the broken ivory tusk and the little black knick-knack box decorated with a Chinese willow pattern.

The dining room was still there with its huge round walnut table. Above the door leading to the area behind the counter was the bell summoning the arrival of a customer. Sandy could taste that box of broken biscuits, feel those crisp lucky bags holding the biggest secret in the world in a little white envelope. And there was the box of greetings cards, some with cardboard records that could actually be played.

Grandpa was probably in the ice house, or maybe refilling an empty vinegar bottle from the barrel.

Sandy's favourite haunt was the secret garden: that was where her spirit returned. The garden was always shaded; marshalled by black pines, and canopied by tall deciduous trees, which allowed only a laser beam of midday sun onto the moss green lawn. It was Sandy's magic garden.

"Penny for 'em, love." Sandy looked up into Bill's kind eyes. She knew how much this was tearing at him. She knew that he wanted to make her happy again after all the problems they had been through.

"I was remembering what the store was like when I was a kid." She smiled, and he sat down beside her on the sofa.

"All happy memories?" Bill squeezed Sandy's hand.

"I was only five when my grandparents had to give up the store, so I don't remember anything other than happy days there."

"That's the best thing, love." Bill kissed her cheek and then raised himself to his feet.

Of course in the grownups' world, things had been very much harder than Sandy had known about for a long time afterwards. In fact, it was only after she had begun researching her family tree that she had learned about the actual location of her grandparents' store, and the history attached to why they let it go. Evidently, her grandparents had wanted Sandy's parents to take it over from them and run it now that they were getting too old for the early mornings and long hours of stocktaking, unpacking and all the wear and tear of a busy business.

Sandy's parents were schoolteachers, and were torn. Teaching was a secure job back in those days, but they had been tempted to jack it all in and run the beloved family store, which had been in the family since 1875. Sandy's research had found that it hadn't always been a grocery store. The first ancestor had sold hats up until the outbreak of the war in 1914, when the shop became an army uniform supplies unit. Between the wars, it became a much-needed second hand clothes store. Then during the next world war, it came into its own when Sandy's grandparents ran the shop as a ration store. Her grandmother explained how everybody was issued with a ration book with a limited number of coupons for all the foods and products folks nowadays took for granted. Nobody was allowed to cheat the system, otherwise Sandy's grandparents would lose their licence. "Although," she remembered her grandmother laughing, and saying, "some folks did try it on, and I had to give them short shrift. One or two posh ones too, who objected to being talked down to by a shop girl."

Another couple had bought the store in the late 1960s, but could not compete with the proliferation of supermarkets. More people could afford cars then, too, and so could drive further afield to shop.

By the mid-Seventies, the shop closed its doors for the last time. A builder had wanted to buy it so he could knock it down to build a block of flats there, but the local residents complained, and eventually a family came from abroad, and bought it, and turned it into a fish and chip shop. From thereon it changed hands a few times throughout the Eighties, Nineties and Noughties. In the second decade of the century it went back to being a grocery store.

Now it was back on the market again.

"I just want to live there," said Sandy to Bill's departing back. "It doesn't matter if it isn't a shop anymore. Please, Bill?"

Bill turned back to face her, smiled that kind smile, and said, "Let me have another think, love, and another look at the maths."

Bill was good at maths. That was why he became an accountant later on in life. He could get his head around those figures others would frown at.

So next time you drive past a house called "The Little Shop" on the corner of the street, don't puzzle as to why there isn't actually a shop there. It's a rather nice home with a blue front door, roses in the front garden, and a newly-retired couple called Sandy and Bill who live there. If you knock on the door, I am sure they would be delighted to tell you the history of that little shop on the corner of the street over a cup of tea and cake.

STACEY'S PLUS ONE

It was Mum who got me into weddings. I think it was because she never had a proper wedding of her own. So she made up for it by becoming an events planner with a strong emphasis on white weddings. She used to take me along to help her lay out the tables, arrange the flowers and favours, and generally be on hand to mop up spills, sew on the occasional loose button, and even now and then act as a shoulder to cry on for disappointed bridesmaids.

Now I have my degree, I have taken over the business administration side of things. Mum and her new partner, Alan, have branched out into complete wedding packages. We even arrange weddings abroad. I don't wish to make you jealous, but we're about to fly out to Cyprus in three weeks for a big wedding party in Paphos. I am teasing you a bit. It's your call. Whatever rocks your boat. A few months ago, a client flew us out to Atlanta for a surfside wedding, which was fabulous in its own way. This was swiftly followed by a Bird of Prey themed do, complete with hawks and owls. I'll leave you to picture how that one went!

Just a minute. I've got a text. It's from Stacey. She's checking that I have everything sorted for Saturday: suit, tie, button-hole, shoes polished, and taxi booked. Now I need to get back to balancing the books. It's a good job I'm used to doing all this, otherwise I would get into a terrible muddle. I couldn't stand the thought of somebody's Big Day being ruined. You only get one shot at this, and you have to get it right.

Sorry, I need to answer another text. This one's from Alice. It's for the Saturday after next. I double-check the entry in my wedding diary. Got it. I text her back. Sorted. Phew. Now back to those books.

Saturday morning I'm up early. Even the birds haven't begun singing yet. I need to wash, shave and get my morning suit on. I checked it last night to make sure there were no wine stains on the front. I'm due to pick up Stacey at ten. Oh, I forgot to mention that I'm going as a wedding guest for this one. Mum and Alan have got another do the other side of the city, so they won't be running things for this one.

I pick up Stacey and we drive to the registry office. Everything is running on time so far. I allowed an extra five minutes because of the roadworks on the corner of the street, but the traffic is quite light today. Perhaps it's because the local football team are playing away today. I hope the groom isn't disappointed at having to miss the match. One wedding I attended had the groom, the best man and the ushers sneaking into the vestry to check on the footie score. The bride looked very cheesed off, I have to say.

Right, that's the register signed. It's a nice little group with a mixture of ages. After a few photos we zoot off to the reception. I am just walking towards the table to sit down when somebody taps me on the shoulder.

"Excuse me. Do I know you from somewhere?"

I turn round and look straight into the angry eyes of a lady who looks a little like my mum, only bigger and fiercer. I really don't recognise this lady at all. Why is she annoyed at me? I don't want to make things awkward for Stacey, so I ask the lady if she would like to step out into the courtyard where we can have a chat.

Thankfully, Stacey has found some friends to talk to, and doesn't appear to notice the mystery lady and yours truly step outside. My heart's thumping a bit. I haven't done anything wrong, but this woman is making me so nervous.

"Young man," she says. "I don't think you are who you say you are." I never said I was anything, but I let her continue. "How long have you known my niece, Stacey?"

I think very carefully before answering this question. If I count the number of weeks since I first spoke to Stacey on the phone, then it is almost four weeks. Yes, nearly one whole month, I realise. So I give her that answer.

"Really?" she says. She is looking me up and down. "Stacey has never mentioned you at all. I didn't even know she had a boyfriend."

Right on cue, Stacey has clocked my predicament and is racing to my rescue.

"Auntie Maisie," she scolds teasingly. "This handsome young man is already taken." Stacey puts her arm through mine and guides me back to the reception table, where the best man is tapping a glass with a pen to get everybody's attention.

All through the reception I try to ignore Auntie Maisie's glowering. I am not sure if she thinks she has seen me at one of the other weddings I have helped at, or is merely curious that her niece just hasn't mentioned who her plus one is. I like Stacey. She has a great sense of humour. By the time we are taking a taxi home, she has already convinced Auntie Maisie that she and I met at another wedding. "Our eyes locked," she said. "And that was that."

That isn't strictly true. Although it's highly likely Stacey could have picked up my business card at a wedding she attended. You see, my other job is acting as plus one to ladies or even gents who don't have anybody to go to weddings with. Most people don't give me the dressing down that Stacey's Auntie Maisie did. I see myself as a prop, quite happy to blend in with the rest of the crowd sharing the special day of two loved ones.

One day I might even meet that special person myself. After all, I am in the right business for looking for love, aren't I?!

SEVEN FOR A SECRET NEVER TO BE TOLD

August 1975. The year I hit my teens. People who are old enough tend to remember the endless summer of '76. I remember instead the previous summer as clearly as cucumber carved up on a cloudfree day near a crate of empty pop bottles. Or a tiding of magpies swooping in for the annual magpie marriage ceremony.

We always wanted to do it all on that first day after Summer Semester. We wanted to clamber on old building sites, stuff our faces with chocolate buns and still be home in time for Doctor Who. I used to think it was my youth, but I know people were less cynical then. We worked and played, kept our secrets away from the ears of infants, and went about our daily lives thankful there wasn't a war on.

That year on the first day of the summer break was when I left our little flat in London to go and stay with my aunt and uncle in Hastings.

When Mum put me on the train, she told me to sit still, read my old *Jackie* magazine and not talk to any strangers, unless it was another mum with kids. A person like her would be safe. Funny how trusting we were back then.

As it was, after I'd waved Mum out of sight, nobody else came and sat with me in my carriage. I liked that. It made me feel suddenly grown-up, rather like a long thread had been snipped and I was off to face the world single-handed. I read the Cathy and Claire page for about the tenth time. And still couldn't agree with the answers they gave to the problems about first kisses and whether or not you should shut your eyes or keep them open. I can't even remember why I kept that old copy of *Jackie*. Maybe I just liked the front cover and didn't want to part with it. Or perhaps it was because we couldn't afford many extras like comics and sweets, it being just the two of us. Some of my mates were going to Spain on holiday. Some had even been to Greek islands, which sounded much too exotic. Mum said they had nasty bugs in those Mediterranean countries. When I told Linda, who was going to Greece for the summer, what my mum had told me, she wouldn't speak to me again.

The train journey seemed to drag on forever. We kept stopping at all these stupid little stations. A few elderly people got on at the first unmemorable one and then dismounted after the next two stops. It seemed a bit pointless. Perhaps they didn't get out much and they came for the ride. After all, it was nice and sunny and they wouldn't want to be cooped up in a stuffy sitting room watching the weatherman explaining how hot it is.

And heck it was hot. I'd tried to open the window, but it was too stiff with dirt and age. So when the ticket collector came to punch a hole in my ticket, I asked him to open the window for me. He was obviously well-practised, because he managed to shunt the whole thing up to the top, and for the rest of the journey I stuck my head as far as I dared out the window to get the breeze to cool me down. That's another thing you couldn't get away with today.

When I stepped off the train in Sussex, it was to realise that I was now all of two inches taller than my recently-retired Uncle, who seemed to have shrunk considerably since the last time I saw him. Auntie Rose looked the same as she had before. Although I think she was using some stuff out of a bottle to keep her hair so blonde. She ran to hug me. And that's when I cried.

"Come on, Sally!" She rubbed my arm. "Pick up her case, will you, Arthur!"

"You alright, love?" he said, and then bent to do her bidding.

She led me to a very old black car that had to be started with Arthur's foot holding the accelerator to the floor.

It was the magpies that started the trouble.

Arthur and I were out in the back garden. He'd been trimming the privet hedge and I was helping him toss the cuttings on to the compost heap. I can't think why the bird picked on him. But just as Arthur bent down to alter the setting on his trimmer, this great big bird dressed in a dinner suit hovered, beak clacking, and then dived for his bald head. It was all over before I could do anything. Arthur just stood there dazed and bleeding from a cut on his temple.

"Little devils," muttered Rose as she sat Arthur down on a wooden kitchen chair and dabbed at his head with disinfectant liquid. "It's been an aggressive breeding season."

I was an urban child and puzzled at the way Rose accepted the bird's wrath, as if it were part of the nature of things and shouldn't be argued with.

Mum always rang each evening at six o'clock, and it was when I was chatting to her about the picnic we'd had on the beach that day the magpie struck again. Only it brought a friend with it this time. Arthur was back by the compost heap and I suddenly heard a terrific rumpus. I asked Mum to hold the line while I went to look out the tiny latticed window of the hallway. Sure enough the magpie was going in for the attack again, while its mate sat and watched, perched on top of the compost.

One for sorrow, two for joy, I thought, and skipped back to finish talking to my mother.

We were now almost half way through the holiday. I was as brown as nutmeg. Auntie Rose was always there with a smile and a jug of cordial.

Mum told me in her next phone call that Linda had sent a postcard from Greece. I was pleased because it meant she still liked me. I was too innocent to realise that she was showing off her exotic location. Hastings, after all, must have seemed very tame to such a globe-trotter.

And then in the last but one week of the holidays before I was due to go back to London, Arthur had his fatal accident. What a strange twist of fate that he was killed outright by an unidentified car, just like my dad had been. Only Dad was on a business trip; Arthur was clobbered as he crossed the road to the off-licence for a bottle of cider.

Mum came down for the funeral the day before I was due to go back to school. The weather was about to break. I remember standing outside in Rose's back garden, watching the angry sky. One by one the magpies came. There were six of them lined up on her privet hedge, screeching and flapping and making a terrible fuss, while she and my mum were trying to put together a wake for the few people who turned up.

As if on cue, I saluted the magpie parliament and recited the magpie rhyme: *One for sorrow, two for joy, three for a girl, four for a boy, five for silver, six for gold, seven for a secret never to be told, eight for a wish, nine for a kiss, ten for a time of joyous bliss.*

The seventh magpie came. He was bigger than the others, and seemed to keep himself a bit apart from them.

"Morning Mr *Magpie*, how's your wife and kids?" I said to him, and turned around on the spot.

He looked at me in a way I'd seen before, opened his beak, and I swear on my father's grave he said: "You alright, love?" Then he ducked his head, flapped his wings and was gone. The others swiftly followed, chanting "Alright, alright, alright."

I watched them disappear into the clouds just as the lightning flashed, and the rain poured down, and washed away my tears.

"Yep," I said. "I'm alright now, Uncle Arthur. Thanks very much."

AUTUMN SUNSHINE

"I hate it now summer's over," said Hannah.

"Look!" said Lucy. "All those birds are lined up along those roofs."

Hannah said, "Yes. They're getting ready to migrate. They'll be flying to some nice sunny place."

Mummy called out, "Everything all right, girls?"

Lucy answered, "No. Hannah's sad about the summer being over."

Mummy said, "Cheer up, Hannah! If we didn't have autumn and winter, then we wouldn't have spring and summer to look forward to."

Hannah said, "Why can't we fly off somewhere warm and sunny like those birds?" As she spoke, suddenly every single bird flew off. Hannah watched the birds out of sight. "I wish it was warm enough to have our paddling pool out just one more time." At that moment rain came pouring out of the sky. "Oh no!" she cried. "Today really must be the last day of summer."

Mummy smiled. "How would you two like to go on a little outing?"

"Yes, please!" chorused the girls.

"Where are we going, Mummy?" asked Lucy, as the girls fastened their seatbelts.

"It's a surprise!" said Mummy.

"Oh, please tell us!" said Hannah.

"You'll just have to wait and see." Mummy reversed the car out on to the road.

"This is exciting!" yelled Lucy.

"Are we nearly there?" asked Hannah.

"Nearly there," said Mummy, turning the car towards the car park. The huge grey building didn't look very exciting.

"Whatever's that, Mummy?" asked Hannah.

"Let's find out," answered Mummy, undoing her seatbelt.

Inside was an indoor tropical rainforest. There were giant lily pads and brightly-coloured flowers. Beautiful birds flew around.

"Look!" said Mummy. "Aren't these birds lucky? They don't have to fly off to find a warmer country."

"Who cares if it's the end of summer!" Hannah laughed. "In here it's summer all year round."

AUTUMN LEAVES

Alice pulled the yellow shawl around her shoulders. A whisper of a draught had chilled her. It must have crept through the gap in the window frame.

She would have to do something about it soon. Before winter crept in. Even though she would be gone from here by then.

Suddenly she spotted movement. Through the misty window she saw the squirrel. She called him Smokey because he was different from the others. A little bigger and definitely a charcoal grey. At first she thought it was a trick of the light and a red squirrel had magicked itself on to the branches of the old ash tree. A dark red squirrel. Or even a hybrid of a grey and a red. But no, she had Googled 'squirrel' and was informed that grey squirrels never teamed up with the reds. They just chased them off. A professor from Cambridge University had written an article explaining that if you look closely at grey squirrel hairs, they are not actually grey at all but are a combination of white, black and orange stripes. The hairs of black squirrels have no stripes. Evidently it was all in the DNA. Alice had failed her Biology exam at school, but knew that even without the scientific explanation, her Smokey was a little bit special. A real beauty.

She had only ever seen a red squirrel once. When she and her late husband Ben had taken a ferry to Brownsea Island. They spent ages searching for them in the pines when somebody yelled that one was eating nuts from the feeder at the island café. What a wonderful holiday that had been. Smokey was scampering up the willow tree now, an acorn clenched between his or maybe her teeth. No, decided Alice. Smokey was a big boy squirrel.

My, she thought. Winter is already here. But I don't remember the summer at all. The Summer of Steve. Somebody special who'd come into her life just at the time when she needed a friend. Somebody to talk to. Somebody who wouldn't ask too many questions.

Smokey darted towards the hedgerow at the back. Soon he was gone. Alice strained to see if she could catch sight of him again. She waited for a few minutes, hoping for another glimpse. One more glimpse of his sleek dark shape and she would be content to get on with packing the rest of her things, ready for the move next week.

But he didn't return.

Feeling saddened, she turned to the kitchen to make herself a cup of coffee. She even took the mug with her, to sip the drink while looking out the window. Surely the squirrel would return.

He had to.

But again she was disappointed.

The phone rang. It was the removal company, asking if she needed any more packing boxes. Alice smiled at the piles of boxes already surrounding her. She couldn't believe how many possessions she'd accumulated, until she'd started emptying all the cupboards and drawers.

Again she thought of Smokey. However did he manage to remember where he hid his acorns?

"No thank you," she said. "I think I have enough. But it's very kind of you to check. I really appreciate it. Goodbye."

Of course, there were some items she would leave in their place until the very last moment of departure.

Including the photo of Ben. It sat on the windowsill of the very window from where she'd first spotted Smokey. Ben. Again she smiled. Ben admitted he wasn't keen on the grey rodents. He said they were pests. Rats with fluffier tails! His grandfather said they were responsible for chasing the reds out of Wales. Dear Ben.

Maybe…she thought to herself, her hand hesitating over the photo frame. But she pulled it back, and, instead, took her empty coffee mug back to the kitchen.

She felt warmer now, and removed her yellow shawl. Draping it over the back of a kitchen chair, she didn't notice the man's shape appear at the front door through the hall off the kitchen. But when the doorbell rang, she knew whose shape it was.

She felt a sudden lifting of her heart. As if a tremendous weight had been removed. She felt light and free-spirited for the first time in so very many months.

"Hello Steve." Alice felt young, kittenish, alive, and so very free.

"Are you ready to let me in to help you?" He looked nervously at all the boxes. "Oh, I see you've nearly done it all." There was no disguising the disappointment in his voice. He'd arrived at the end of the packing party.

"Steve! Of course. Thank you. I could do with some help. You are a Godsend." She stepped aside to let him in. "I'll make you a coffee. Don't suppose you know anything about removing gaps in window frames?" She tried not to sound too foolish.

"Now that's something I can help you with!" He looked two inches taller. "I've got my tool bag in the van. I'll get it." But before he did, he picked up the precious photo. "Best put this in a safe place before I start work on the frame, though." Alice took it from him and placed it on a table, ready for wrapping and packing away. When she turned to look at him again, though, his back was turned. He was staring at something outside.

Steve said, "Alice, is that a dark red—"

"No. It's Smokey. He's charcoal grey. Sometimes they come out that way."

"How incredible." Steve whipped out his smartphone and managed to capture a picture of Smokey. "I'll WhatsApp the photo to you, so you don't forget us when you are in your new home."

Alice smiled and stood shoulder-to-shoulder with Steve, watching with wonder.

ANNIVERSARY

It was going to be another beautiful day. Just as yesterday had been and the day before that. Unlike the Mediterranean playgrounds, Northern Europe has to count each and every hot summer day as precious— as precious as Welsh gold and kind hearts. After all, who knew what storms might be waiting round the corner? Well, decided Cora with a little laugh, the weatherman ought to be getting that one right!

She watched the river birds. There were more this year. Hadn't she heard somewhere that spring is arriving a month early each year? So did that mean the first day of spring should be celebrated on the 21st February instead of the 21st day of March? Her mother would disapprove, after all, she had met Cora's father on the first day of spring. An anniversary she would never forget. So many days, so many anniversaries, however do we keep up with it all?

At that moment, two ducks were squabbling over another duck, and an even bigger bird—was it a goose?—had climbed out on to the bank and was making an awful tooting sound. They never used to behave like this when she was a little girl. And as for those seagulls, there seemed to be as many inland these days as on the beach. Perhaps they were fed up with having to pick their way through all that plastic washed up on the shoreline. Picnickers and office folk snatching a quick break provided easier pickings now the local councils were covering over all the beach bins. Messy things, gulls. But they never used to be this way, Cora decided. People were brushing themselves down and heading back to work. Lunchtime was over. Unless you were a duck!

*   *   *

Cora's high-heeled shoes clicked loudly as she hurried down the High Street. There was no need to rush, she had no plane to catch or meeting to attend. At least, she could not think of any reason for hurrying.

Cora was always in a hurry and always had been.

Unlike her best friend, Anna, she could not tolerate hold-ups or slowness in people and machines. She dashed through life always forgetting to do things and sometimes ending up having to go back to finish things off properly. Anna, on the other hand, was a plodder, steady and reliable.

Suddenly, Cora stopped dead in her tracks nearly causing the man behind her to bump into her. He muttered something under his breath and skated deftly round her.

"What on earth have I done with my handbag?" She turned and ran across the road right in the path of an oncoming vehicle. The driver screeched to a halt, stuck his head out of the window and shouted an obscenity at Cora.

She did not hear him because she did not want to hear him. She had developed an uncanny way of blocking out anything she did not want to associate herself with. She referred to it as her "emotional deadness".

Right now all she was concerned about was getting back her handbag. She wanted to get to it before someone else did. She was especially apprehensive as both her cheque book and cheque card were in it. She had worked in a bank for a while and knew that she should not carry them both together - though everybody did.

She ran up the steps of the Post Office two at a time, her auburn hair fanning out behind her like a flame on a windy day. She squeezed her narrow frame between two elderly gentlemen who had decided to share a cigarette and a chat in the warm. A frantic scan of the building and luck was on her side this time: there it was tucked away in the farthest corner. Now she remembered putting it there as she stuck stamps to some envelopes.

A sigh of relief as she zipped open the bag to check all was intact, she told herself to calm down and take a few deep breaths..."Oh God!" It was one o'clock and she was supposed to have met Anna at twelve.

I could cry now, only I never cry. But if I did cry this would be the time to do it.

Anna would understand. They hadn't made any definite arrangements anyway. Anna knew better than to do that. Cora had told her she wasn't certain she would be able to get today off. She really wanted to try and make it.

Anna had been her best friend at school and college. In the intervening years though, their differing careers and lifestyles meant they did not see so much of each other.

Anna had been working in Stockholm for the past six months: she detested the travelling and, unlike Cora, longed to settle down. Anna had not had very much luck in her personal relationships: the previous one had lasted two years and ended abruptly. Cora worried about her sweet, jolly little friend. She hoped she would soon meet someone who would be worthy of her.

As Cora made her way towards the swing doors leading on to the High Street, she happened to catch the glance of a young man - late twenties, casually yet smartly dressed, dark hair, well-cut, attractive, yet not too aware of himself. They both looked shyly away as strangers do when they fear being caught staring.

Something made Cora look back again. He seemed familiar. It was the turquoise eyes, the way they tilted down slightly at the corners. She had always had a weakness for eyes like that. Whenever she saw a man with those eyes it reminded her of ... him. Surely this could not be him though?

The eyes aside, this man was different: shorter, stockier. True, he looked about the right age. The hair also was straighter, darker. Cora was unsure.

The young man had time to get through the doors without appearing rude if he'd just let them swing behind him. Yet he stood there holding the door as if deliberately waiting for her to come through.

An elderly woman limped painfully in front of her. Cora tried not to think about growing old and being unable to take care of herself; always waiting for some grandchild or other to phone or visit, and always complaining about aches and pains or the cost of everything. No, Cora decided. If I am fortunate enough to grow old then I will endeavour to be one of those cheery grandmas they show in children's stories. Grandmas who smile a lot, and are kind and hand out plenty of sweets when the parents' backs are turned.

She watched as the young man ensured the lady was safely through the doorway. Is it or isn't it *him*? She was so sure it was and yet was she?

She was pleased he was still holding the door open for her, too. She could not remember the last time anyone had done this for her. She was so used to barging her way through life like everyone in the crowd; frequently a door would swing in her face unless she ran to catch it.

As she passed through the doorway, hazel eyes met turquoise eyes for a fraction of a second and then no more. She muttered "Thank you" and continued walking down the steps on to the High Street.

She felt a little embarrassed as he was still looking at her as if he wanted to say something, but could not pluck up the courage.

She thought: No, I do not know you, but if you think you know me then why don't you say something? Surely to goodness you've conquered that stupid shyness now?

She watched him dart through the traffic towards the building society.

But then that was just like you, you always stared at me but were too shy even to say hello. Of course I blamed myself too. I was just a kid as well. You should have, could have made the first move.

You're good-looking enough. But there was something more: I really believed if I could win you then I would need to search no more. My whole life would have revolved around you and your brilliant career. You were clever all right. Too intelligent by far. Maybe there was something more. Maybe I was jealous of you. Yes, of you my darling who never was. Is this what they call destiny?

The stranger had gone. Cora felt moved, uneasy, uncertain. The silence, like a great barrier, still separated them.

She saw an empty telephone kiosk. May as well get it over with. She was still feeling guilty about the lunch date. But as all good friends they would quickly iron out any grievances.

Was it really six months since they'd seen each other? So much can happen in that time. Cora had even heard a rumour that Anna was thinking about getting engaged. Maybe this would be the right one at last.

Cora wished she saw her friends more often. Her temping put her all over the place. Not that she complained, as it suited her temperament and personality: always on the move, life unpredictable, no danger of her roots being firmly planted. Cora was too independent for that.

Having dialled Anna's number and let it ring about a dozen times, she replaced the receiver and then tried again in case she'd misdialled. No reply.

Oh, well, I'll just have to try again when I get home. It's a good job she knows me well enough to understand my flippancy. No doubt she'll have guessed something cropped up and I let her down again.

A sudden emptiness came over her. It was like the feeling one sometimes gets when one had had a head cold and goes out in the chilly morning air for the first time.

Cora smiled, cynically thinking: Now, don't get sentimental, old girl, these are hunger pangs.

She marched straight to the nearest burger joint for a quarter-pounder with cheese and an ice-cold chocolate milkshake in all its clinical, pre-packaged, polystyrene glory.

How she loved to treat herself to this. It beat all the posh restaurants she never got invited to. That is what she kept telling herself anyway. Yes, Miss Independent she was now, and so she would always be.

Yet why had that feeling of emptiness come back in spite of a now full stomach?

Hard she was, hard to herself, hard to others. If anybody did not come up to scratch they were dismissed from her life. Yes, even he obviously did not come up to scratch. Yet the hunger lingered on.

She left the fast food outlet in a half dream world. For the first time in years she was suddenly looking at people. Yes, people. At last they had personalities, feelings, worries and cares. No longer were they the blurry objects that she hurried past on her way to the office, or on her way home. Each tiny child was a miniature version of the adult it would one day grow to be. Will he be successful? Will she be lucky in love?

Surely that old ache could not be returning after all these years?

She found herself staring in the window of the main department store at the new range of autumn dresses. The window dresser was still arranging them and smiled at Cora. Cora returned her smile and then saw her reflection in the glass: a tired, lonely woman who has just seen a ghost from the past.

Returning to where she still lived with her parents, she was unable to shake him from her mind. She got annoyed with herself. There was no time for this depressive feeling. She had suffered long and hard from melancholia after leaving college all those years ago. She had left a part of herself behind: a part of her very soul.

For six months after leaving she had found it hard to laugh at things; there were times when for no reason she would burst into tears causing embarrassment to herself and others.

She withdrew into herself and so the pain lingered. But Cora was strong-minded and strong-willed. She had picked up the threads of her emotions and pitched into life as a free agent. She vowed she would never cry again.

Unable to decide on a specific career, she shopped around doing courses in secretarial practice, book-keeping, even creative writing. After jumping through several jobs she signed up for agency work. This gave her all the variety she craved for in a career. Though it did not allow her the security to purchase her own home.

Cora had had some good times, good laughs since leaving college. She reflected on those years which had flowed past like the sun-dappled river which ran through her home town.

She could see the river from her bedroom. As a child she would watch it for hours. She especially loved the power of it when there had been a heavy rain. Then it would gush past, carrying interesting bits of debris: old cans, branches, pieces of metal. It would ferry these little souvenirs of life's experiences for miles and miles, then drop them, discard them on a strange bank, flowing onwards towards the open sea and freedom. Freedom from the cares of the dirty old towns, and tired villages kept alive only by the incessant gossip of their inhabitants.

Cora was tired of her home town. It was time to spread her wings: she had built up this wall of confidence; confidence always being some-thing she had lacked as a teenager.

She was ready to make it on her own; away from family and close friends. Yet her wings felt shaky and unsure, like those of a young bird making its first flight. But it dare not hesitate or falter, for to do so would mean certain death or being left behind to starve while the brave ones flew on to sunnier climes.

Cora went up into the attic. Sitting among her old books and other remnants of her lost youth was like a journey back in time.

She picked up an old picture book, and turning the pages, now yellowed with damp and age, she reflected upon the time she and her mother went to buy this book. How excited she was: her first reading book. She loved the smell of new books. Now it smelt musty.

As she sorted through the box of old toys, she came across some of the last pieces of work she had done before leaving college. Was it really so long ago? Picking up an old photograph album, she wiped the dust from its cover and turned the leaves. There was a group photograph of her primary school class.

Anna was there, blonde, pig-tailed and innocent as a baby doll; Cora was sitting cross-legged and looking shyly at the camera.

Good gracious! How skinny and elfin-like I was then, and of course, he was there. She smiled as she thought of the role that they had all played in each other's lives...The phone rang, jolting Cora out of her dream world.

Back to her normal self, she dashed downstairs in four leaps, snatched up the receiver, breathlessly repeating the number.

"Sorry, Cora! It's only me! Did you think it was your secret lover phoning to ask you to come away for a romantic weekend in Venice? Or maybe a day trip to Stockholm would be more your style?" There was a fit of giggles at the other end. "Well I had to think of some excuse for you not turning up at lunchtime. Okay, you're forgiven again! Anyway, as it happens, after you hadn't turned up I went home and as I was turning the key in the lock I heard the phone ringing. So I ran in, picked it up and it was guess who? Oh wait a minute, I haven't told you, have I? Today I got engaged!"

"Congratulations! Who was it on the phone then?"

"Why, him of course!"

"Go on!"

"He said we should buy the ring this afternoon!"

"Now tell me who this lucky chap is then? Anybody I know?"

"Well, actually, you may recall him from ages back when we were at college. Do you remember a guy called Peter Harford? Well anyway he remembers you from school. We were having a bit of a laugh the other night, swapping notes about old flames and all that. Anyhow, he said that when we were at college he had a tremendous crush on you, but was too scared to ask you out. Still he says I'm the only woman for him now. So hands off! You know how much I've always wanted to get married. I nearly went to pieces when I split up with Neil, remember?"

"Yes, I remember..." Cora was half-dazed. "I was always the one who wanted to stay independent. You hated being single."

"That was all long ago, Cora. Thank goodness. I'm sorry to keep going on about it, but being in love really is the greatest thing. I know you enjoy your freedom, Cora, but you can't be on the move all your life. Isn't it time you thought about finding someone to settle down with? Is there anyone special at the moment? By the way, how's work?"

"Okay."

"Oh yes, I forgot to tell you the rest of the story..." Anna had more effervescence than a bottle of champagne. "Now where did I get to? Oh, yes, anyway it was Peter on the phone as I'm sure you've gathered. He said he wanted to meet me as soon as possible so that we could go and buy the ring. He told me he'd just been round to the building society to draw out the money to buy it. Isn't that sweet? Oh, Cora, he's so gorgeous. He's changed a lot since he left college. He's not so skinny now. Remember how skinny he was at college? I don't think I would have given him a second look then. Mind you, remember how fat I was then? And the acne. Oh gosh, I'd never want to live through those days again. I went on more diets than I watched episodes of *Dallas*. Anyway must dash, got loads of people to phone, oh, and Cora, look after yourself, there's a love, bye now! Oh, I nearly forgot, Cora, do you realise that it was eleven years ago today we left college? Doesn't it make you feel old? It is quite an anniversary isn't it?"

Anna rabbited on for several more minutes, saying goodbye at least another six times before finally hanging up. Cora had never heard anybody so happy and rightly so. She placed the receiver very quietly down and tiptoed back upstairs to the attic.

She calmly sat down; holding the photo album gently to her, she felt the tears running down her face.

* * *

At the time, decided Cora, those tears were bitter and heart-breaking. She thought she loved Peter more than Anna did. Perhaps she had in a way. Although, if she were to step outside of herself and try to view it from another person's perspective, it was more the *idea* of loving Peter that was appealing than the practicalities of an actual relationship. This strategy was another piece of advice she had heard or read somewhere. Her head was full of it. But then she had been around for a long time for all this wisdom to accumulate.

Cora had never married, but she had been godmother to Anna and Peter's children, and she had been there for Anna when Peter was cruelly snatched away by cancer. Now Anna too had been gone a number of years.

"Nanna Cora?"

"Yes, darling?"

"Shall we push you inside now? Mummy says she is ready with the birthday cake." Little Cora junior was fishing around in her godmother's pockets.

"No more sweeties until after tea," whispered Cora senior.

"But—"

"All right, just one. But make sure you brush your teeth well to-night. Promise?"

"I promise, Nanna Cora. And Nanna Cora?"

"Yes, darling?"

"Are you really eighty-seven today?"

"So they tell me, darling. But then who's counting?"

With that a group of godchildren and great-godchildren - if there was such a thing - fluttered round her like busy little birds, pushing her into the tearoom with - as a centrepiece - the biggest most beautiful rainbow cake Cora had ever seen in her life!

MUSICAL SHOWTIME

"Dad! Dad!" screamed Emily. "They're having a holiday guests' show on the main stage tonight. You have to sing!"

"But I haven't sung in front of an audience since 1987." Simon stunned himself with the sudden realisation that those years since his teens had whizzed by, and he was now the father of a very lively teenager.

"And won't you be embarrassed to see your old Dad up there, strutting his stuff?" threw in Mum.

"Nah! I grew out of that years ago. It'd be great to see Dad on stage having fun. We'll rescue him if the audience start flinging items of lingerie or worse at him."

"Eat yer heart out, Tom Jones." Mum sniggered. "But yeah, why not have a go, Si? It's only a bit of fun. And it is our last night. Tomorrow we'll be back to work." She looked a little glum at the thought.

"Don't remind me of the garage. The daily grind will come round soon enough. The flight home always seems quicker than the flight out," he mused. Then, "Okay, I'll do it!"

"Hooray!" shouted Mum and Emily.

The hardest bit was finding something for Simon to sing.

"I was a New Romantic," said Si, scanning the list of songs he could choose from.

"More like Old Romantic." Mum laughed. When he looked at her moodily, she swallowed a giggle and said, "Sorry, love."

But yes. In his heyday he'd twanged the strings of many a teenage heart with his renditions of Spandau Ballet's 'True' and Duran Duran's 'Girls on Film'. Mum remembered having to elbow aside many an adoring fan. Indeed she was quite relieved when he finally gave up on his dreams of popstardom and became a garage mechanic instead.

At least she got to see him every night after work. And he didn't have to go touring to these ghastly little smoky venues up and down the country anymore. No, now he repaired the vehicles that transported other wannabe stars.

"This is the selection of backing tracks we can use for the contestants," said the helpful rep. "As you can see, there's plenty of ABBA, Beatles and Oasis tracks." She looked Si up and down and added, "How about a bit of Robbie Williams?"

Mum looked the young rep up and down and said, "No. I don't think Si's quite got the legs for Robbie."

"Really?" said Si, looking hurt. "I could try 'Angels' perhaps?"

"No," said Mum. "You are definitely no angel. But there must be a suitable Beatles track for you. Everybody loved the Beatles."

Si eventually decided on 'Yesterday'.

He was allowed a couple of practice runs before the show began. Before him was a bunch of teenage guys who were doing a rap song. Si thought he recognised it as being one of Eminem's. Although he quite liked the song, he thought they were doing a terrible job of it.

Unfortunately, one of the teenagers saw him laughing at them, and when their performance was over, he approached Si: "Oy! Old man," he said. "What was so funny?"

"Nothing," said Si. He was anxious to get away, as he was now due on stage.

"Was he poking fun at us?" said one of the other lads, keen to get in on the action.

"No!" said Si. "Now would you please move aside. I'm the next performer."

"So what are you gonna sing, Old Man?" said the first youngster again.

"'Yesterday' by the Beatles," answered Si, heading towards the stage. "Figures," said the youngster. "Must be about your era. The Sixties.""I'll have you know I was a New Romantic!" retorted Si.

"Right. So where's the mullet then?" The young man pointed at Si's bald head. They all burst out laughing.

Si decided he didn't want to go up on stage now. He was feeling annoyed, and nervous and worried they would boo him off. But as he turned to go, Emily and Mum appeared.

"What's up, Si?" said Mum.

"Oh, those young guns are giving me a bit of hassle," he said.

Emily grinned and said, "Actually, I've been seeing one of them on the quiet." She winked across at the boys, and then pointed at Si. "Give the old man a chance," she said.

"Does he need a backing group?" said the one of the boys.

"Well, Dad?"

They waited for him to reply.

Si looked thoughtful and said, "No. I've had a change of mind. And I'd like to change the tune." He spotted the rep organising the show, and went over to speak to her.

The act that was supposed to follow Si went on ahead of him. It was a girl-band formed by three of the friendliest, liveliest mums on the holiday resort. They did a comical rendering of Girls Aloud's 'Sound of the Underground'. The ladies received a thunderous applause and standing ovation from the boy band Si had been tittering at.

But before Si could decide if it was a conspiracy, he realised the fading of the final cry of approval meant that he was the final act.

And when he came on, he sang a wonderful, albeit unrehearsed rendition of 'My Way'. The audience was spellbound. Even a member of the boy band looked as if he had a tear in his eye.

Later, after a thunderous applause, Mum ran over to him and said, "You are an Old Romantic after all."

And they kissed in the moonlight on their last night of the holiday.

CAN'T COOK, CAN PLAY DARTS

Everybody's got something they're good at, haven't they? I may manage to make bangers and mash look like last week's leftovers, but I can throw a bullseye with just the blinking of an eye. I'm not bragging, believe me.

My mum-in-law thought I should stay at home and practise baking blind or cooking something without charcoaling it. I was quite happy to live on takeaways and stock up on all these 'buy-two-get-one-free' TV dinners which I could whack into the freezer. Even if I'd wanted to improve my culinary skills, I just didn't have the time. I was on a roll. I was working my way up to the National Championships. Nobody was going to stop me.

It's not as if my husband, Guy, didn't know about my darts playing. We actually met at a darts tournament. We were playing in rival teams, his office against mine. He didn't seem to mind that my team beat his; truly slaughtered them. He congratulated me, bought me a drink, drove me home, and the rest was history.

When we married I didn't exactly scream out for a dart-shaped wedding cake. In fact, during that first week of our honeymoon I found myself - rather foolishly - saying I'd try harder with my cooking, if he'd put the same effort into learning D-I-Y.

But later, when the honeymoon was over, I was itching to get back to my darts.

When I announced I intended pursuing my darts career, Guy went quiet, but his mother hit the roof. "You're a married woman now, Tina," she snorted. "Darts matches are for beer-bellied, chain-smoking males."

I looked to Guy for support, but he'd already got his nose stuck in a

D-I-Y manual. After she'd gone, I reluctantly flicked through the cook book which had come with my new oven. I'd start with something simple like an omelette.

Just as I was nervously cracking an egg, the phone rang. Guy answered it. "It's your mate, Helen," he muttered, plonking the receiver down on the hall table. "I'm off down the pub for a quick pint. Then I'm going to get cracking on decorating the spare bedroom."

Helen sounded very excited. "You must come to the next darts evening," she screeched. "There's going to be a television crew there. Evidently somebody's doing a documentary on role-reversal."

"So what had darts got to do with it?" I asked puzzled.

"Darts was traditionally a man's game. You know. Beer bellies and smoky pubs. That sort of thing."

Now where had I heard that before?

I'm no fool. I leapt at the opportunity of appearing on telly. But how was I going to manage to get away with it without Guy, and more importantly his mother finding out?

I told Helen my dilemma. Being a woman, she came up trumps, of course. "Tell him you and me are going to cookery lessons."

What a doll she is! "See you Tuesday!" I shouted with delight.

True to his word, Guy had his quick pint and was soon letting himself back in the front door. When I told him Helen and I were going to learn how to cook properly, he gave me one of those silly grins which usually preceded him sweeping me up into his arms and staggering up the stairs with me. This time he made a grab for the paint pot and brushes and staggered up the stairs with them instead.

Tuesday evening came, and I was just snatching up my car keys when Guy piped up from the armchair in front of his favourite TV programme, "You don't look as if you're going to a cookery lesson, Tina. Where are your ingredients? My sister used to have to take loads of stuff, flour, that sort of thing."

I stopped dead. Oh, no. He'd found me out. Then I had a brainwave. "It's just theory tonight. The teacher is going to do a demonstration. That's why I don't need to take anything."

I was about to dart out the door - sorry about the pun - when Guy jumped up from the chair and said, "Tell you what, love. I'll give you a lift. I wasn't too happy with the way the engine sounded this morning. I'd hate you to break down in the dark."

That was it. My cover was blown. He'd guessed, of course. Then I had a brainstorm. "Oh thanks, love. Tell you what. Just drop me off at Helen's. We were going to go in her car anyway."

I'm lucky Guy is slow on the uptake and Helen is very quick- witted. As soon as she saw us arrive, she guessed I was working on a decoy. She even managed to charmingly persuade my husband she'd drive me home.

"Phew!" I breathed a sigh of relief as she and I drove off to the darts match and that exciting TV documentary filming, which went superbly.

I'm sorry to say my cooking didn't improve. Well how could it when I was playing darts every Tuesday evening instead of brushing up on my shortcrust pastry? Guy suggested I ask the cookery teacher for a refund. Then when the documentary was due to be shown on television, I knew I had to come clean. I braced myself for a terrible scene when I told Guy the truth and nothing but the truth.

"You daft thing." He laughed, wrapping his arms around me. "I hadn't guessed about the telly bit, but of course I knew what you were getting up to."

"And you're not mad at me?" I said, not knowing whether to laugh or cry.

"'Course not. Now let's watch this documentary."

And in case you're wondering: I won the National Championships. After seeing me on the telly, even Guy's mum rallied round to cheer me on! Soon I'll be having to defend my title.

And Guy? Good old, darling old Guy. He's revelling in my success. Oh, and he sure cooks a mean omelette!

CONFIDING IN GRAN

Oh, heck. Is that the time? I'd better be getting back to the office. Mind you, this watch gains a bit. By the time I need to forward it or wind it back an hour, it's usually gained about five minutes.

Time. It's a funny old thing, isn't it? Standing at a draughty bus-stop for even two minutes seems precious time painfully wasted. Yet getting up for work two minutes late often means no breakfast, no time to open the post, and that same old bus trundling off down the road without you.

Not that it's a problem for you any more, is it? You've got all the time in the world, haven't you? Thanks for listening to me rabbiting on, by the way. I've got no one else at the moment to share my problems with. Mum's got herself a new boyfriend, would you believe? Only three years older than Yours Truly.

"Mum," I said, as she was making the last minute adjustments to her already perfect salon-highlighted hair. "Mum? Why don't you stay in for once? It's no good burning the candle at both ends, you know!"

And do you know what she said? "Carrie," she twittered. "You're just jealous 'cos you can't get yourself a nice fella!"

Me? Jealous of my old Mum?

"Give over," I said. "I haven't got to the stage yet where I'm desperate to go out with anyone who gives me a second look."

Then she marched off in my high-heels, wearing my little black number, thank you very much, slammed the door, and she and lover-boy zoomed off in a cloud of gravel. Heaven knows what the neighbours must think. Still, thankfully I haven't got to the stage where I worry what the neighbours think either.

It's not that I resent Mum going out. She's had her share of being stuck in for one reason or another. And I don't need to tell you that folks are a long time dead, do I?

Right. That's it. I really must prise myself off this damp old bench and find some enthusiasm for returning to my desk; which is bound to be covered in those ghastly little yellow stick-ons, each sporting the telephone number of those individuals who are daft enough to ring me during the lunch hour. You were lucky enough not to experience the ups and downs of office life. What an interesting life you had! When you used to tell me about those exciting times you had as a young teacher during the Fifties, I admit I used to switch off. I never let on I wasn't listening, did I? Even though I was young and selfish, I didn't want to hurt your feelings. I loved you too much for that.

Now I regret not paying more attention to what you were saying. I saw an advertisement in the local paper asking for people's own personal memories of the Fifties. You could have filled a book, couldn't you? I wish I'd written it all down. It would have been a way of hanging on to your memory somehow. I still miss you so much.

I hope you like the flowers I brought you today. Yellow roses. They're Mum's favourites. Again, because I never paid enough attention, I can't remember what your favourite flowers were. Perhaps you preferred to see them growing, rather than clipped off in their prime and stuck in a vase for a slow lingering death.

Sorry. I shouldn't have said that. Still, looking at the funny side of things, I hope nobody's heard me nattering on to you. Not that many people visit this cemetery during lunchbreaks. It's quite a walk from the High Street. And even on a sunny June day like this, it's not the ideal place to have some fun, is it? A lot of the graves are so overgrown, I doubt anybody comes to visit them. It's sad. Yet people's lives are so hectic these days. Look at Mum, for instance. Who'd have thought she'd start acting like a teenager again? There again, if you were still around, she wouldn't be, would she?

"She's missing your dad," I can almost hear you say.

Right. My borrowed five minutes are up. I really must say goodbye now. It was nice talking to you. I'll come back and see you again soon, I promise. Unless I suddenly find myself in the midst of a social whirl, like Mum. I doubt it somehow. I mean, just look. I've even been stood up here today.

I thought he'd come. I hoped he'd come.

Okay. Up I get. Now it's back to the office. Wait a minute. There's somebody coming through the lychgate.

"Hi Dad!"

"Hello Carrie. So sorry I'm late. A bit hectic in the office, you know?"

I know. But at least he's here!

Even though he's my dad, I'm tongue-tied. "Here," I say. "I got you a card and present."

"But it's not my birthday." His handsome, still-unlined face looks puzzled.

"I know it's not your birthday, silly." I smile. "It's for Sunday." "Sunday?" That puzzled look just won't go away.

"Yes. Sunday's Father's Day. Remember?"

He kisses my cheek. He's avoiding my gaze. I think there are tears in his eyes. I know there are tears in mine.

"I've just been talking to Gran," I say, feeling childish and silly.

Dad puts his arm round my shoulders. "And what did she have to say to you, love?" he asks gently.

"She says she wishes you and Mum could be friends again." I

almost wince as the words come out of my mouth. It's like it's not really me speaking. It's almost spooky, like Gran is talking through me.

"Know something?" He smiles. "I think Gran's right. Life's too short to quarrel."

"So you'll come round on Sunday then?"

"Yes. And another thing..."

"What?"

"Yellow roses were your Gran's favourite." He looks thoughtful before adding, "And your Mum's."

"I know, Dad." I link my arm through his. It's a beautiful summer's day, and a great day to be alive.

Thanks Gran.

SCHOOL BREAK

"It's so unfair!" Ali said. "Judi and Kim have gone away for the school holiday." She looked at her mum sadly. "Why can't we go away, too?"

"Because Dad's on a course."

"I wish we were going away this week," Ali moaned. "It's going to be horrid without my friends around."

"Don't worry, Ali. I'm sure you'll find lots to do."

"Like what?" Ali frowned.

"Shopping with me. A visit to the library. And there's always the playground."

Ali brightened a little when her mum mentioned the playground. But her excitement ended when she switched on the television and saw the weather forecast.

"Oh, Mum! It's going to rain. We can't go to the playground now!"

"Let's go to the library instead," said Mum.

They went in the car. Both Ali and Mum chose some library books. As they came out of the library they felt a few raindrops.

"Quick!" said Mum. "Let's get back to the car before the rain gets really heavy."

At home Ali settled down to read her books. She was enjoying an exciting adventure story so much, that at first she didn't hear her mum calling from downstairs

"Ali!" called Mum. "Ali! It's stopped raining. It's lovely outside now! How about we go to the playground?"

"I'm coming, Mum!" shouted Ali. "That's a great book I got out the library."

Ali was busy telling her mum about the story as they walked to the playground. She didn't notice the girl with the blonde plaits who was playing by the swings.

"Look!" said Mum. "That girl looks about your age. Do you know her?"

"No," said Ali. "She doesn't go to my school."

"Why don't you go over and talk to her?" coaxed Mum. "She looks a bit lonely."

So Ali went up to the girl. "Hi! I'm Ali. Do you live near here?"

"Hello." The girl smiled. "I'm Katy. We've just moved into that house over there." Katy pointed to a house which was very close to the playground.

"Does that mean you'll be going to Hillbank school?" asked Ali. The girl grinned. "Yes. I'm going to be in Miss Smith's class."

"Miss Smith is my teacher," said Ali excitedly.

"I really miss my friends," said Katy.

"My friends, Judi and Kim, are both away on holiday," said Ali. "I'm missing them too."

Katy shyly asked, "Would you like to play with me?"

"Yes!" said Ali. "You can tell me all about your friends and I'll tell you about mine."

The girls chatted. Mum came over to say hello. "How about we introduce ourselves to your mum, Katy?"

Katy's mum was really pleased to meet Ali and her mum.

"We had to move house so quickly," she said to Ali's mum. "That we didn't have chance to arrange for Katy to visit her new school." She invited Ali and her mum in for a cup of tea.

"Ali's dad is on a course this week," said Ali's mum. "Otherwise we might have gone away. Both Ali's friends are away. Ali's missing them."

"Yes," said Katy's mum. "Katy's missing her friends, too."

"Where are Ali and Katy, by the way?" asked Ali's mum.

They heard happy voices coming from Katy's bedroom.

Katy's mum smiled. "It sounds like Ali and Katy have both made a new friend!"

WE'RE ALL GOING ON A CYBER-HOLIDAY!

Tammy felt very miserable. She wanted to go home. It was so unfair. Dad said he would buy them both a comic when they got to the airport. But even this didn't cheer her up.

"Please, Dad," said Tammy for the fifth time.

"No," said Dad. "I'm not turning this car round and going back. We'll miss the plane!"

"But, Dad, if we don't go back now, my cyber-pet will turn into an alien and fly off into space."

"Well, it won't be the first time," said her brother, Matt. "You never look after it properly." He was playing with his toy tiger.

"I do so!" Tammy cried.

"No, you don't," Matt shouted back.

"Yes I do. Anyway, where's your cyber-pet, Smarty-pants?" Tammy was close to tears.

"I've booked mine into a hotel," boasted Matt.

"Show-off!" she yelled. "It's going to be a horrid, horrid holiday."

"It will be, with you moaning all the time," said her brother, cuddling the tiger. "Look! I can see an aeroplane taking off. I can't wait to get on the plane."

"We've got to check our baggage in first," said Mum. "Then we'll have time to buy those comics."

Tammy stared out of her window. She was still thinking about her cyber-pet. He was probably sitting on her dressing-table beeping for her. Or had she really left him on her dressing table? Anyway, wherever he was, he was probably hungry, lonely and needed playing with.Dad drove into the long-stay car-park at the airport. The family took their cases out of the boot. Mum and Dad checked all the car windows were closed and that the doors were locked properly. Then Matt said, "Oh no!" He had lost his cuddly tiger.

Mum unlocked the door. Dad found the tiger on the floor. "Come on! Let's go!" said Dad.

Soon the family were checking in their luggage.

"Right. Let's go and choose those comics," said Dad, pointing to the newsagents.

As they were paying for the comics, they all heard a loud beeping noise.

"That must be the cash-till," said Dad.

"It sounded just like my cyber-pet," shouted Tammy. "And it seems to be coming from your jacket pocket, Dad." As quick as a flash Tammy dived for Dad's pocket and pulled out the pink cyber-pet. "Oh, look. He needs cleaning up. I'd better do it right away." She pressed all the right buttons.

"And perhaps that'll teach you to look after him better," said Dad.

"Yes," said Mum, coming up behind them. "Look, Matt! You left your cuddly tiger in the shop."

Dad looked serious and said, "Both of you must take care of your things."

Tammy's cyber-pet beeped again. She said, "I wonder what he wants now?" Again she pressed the right buttons. "Coming, Dad! Thanks so much for bringing my cyber-pet. I promise I'll look after him."

Dad smiled and said, "Come on! Let's go and have a great holiday!"

UNICORNS

"Is it true about the Unicorns?" Jenny's long-lashed blue eyes were looking up at me.

"What?" I answered, trying so hard not to let the edginess sound in my voice.

Jenny climbed up into my lap and lay her head on my shoulder. "Is it true they were too busy playing in the sea to hear Noah calling them?" She was fighting the urge to stick her thumb into her mouth, an old comforter from infancy. "And then they were swept away?" she sighed sadly.

"I don't remember that," I lied, feeling such a fraud, and yet my mind was so solidly fixed on another more urgent matter. I turned to look at my mother's pale face, and pleaded with her with my tired eyes.

With the advantage of maturity, she came up trumps: "Oooh, yes, Jenny." She smiled, and put on her best cookies-and-milk voice. "I remember the song about the Unicorns."

Jenny slid off my lap and ran to her grandmother's open arms. My mother helped her to climb up and sat with her, stroking her head gently as she struggled to recall the song we loved listening to in happier times. "I can remember the tune, but I can't remember the singer."

I detected a waiver in her voice.

"The Bachelors," replied my father huskily. "Cor, that takes me back, sixty-five, sixty-six. Oooh, sometime about then."

It occurred to me that it was rather ironic a song about Unicorns was so popular during an era of sex, drugs and rock 'n' roll.

Mum started singing it and Dad hummed along weakly. I always used to laugh at my parents' harmonies when I was younger. Now I felt like crying.

"Were they really the loveliest of them all?" Jenny's eyes were shining.

"'Course they were - ouch!" Dad winced, Mum stopped singing and held Jenny closer to her. She watched helplessly as his grey head sank back into the hospital pillow. "'Course they were, love," he whispered and closed his eyes.

Mum and I eyed one other, each wondering whether a nurse should be summoned. Then Jenny burst into tears.

"What is it, lass?" Dad opened an eye. The pain must have subsided for now.

She sobbed, "So I'll never, never, never get to see one then. Never, ever, ever?"

My mother was struggling to open her handbag to find a tissue. Dad stared up at me. How much do you tell a six-year-old? Albeit a very bright six-year-old, with a reading age of eight? Yet in some ways Jenny seemed younger than six. A very early talker but always a very clingy child. Should I tell her the truth about the Unicorns? Or should I let her believe in them? There again, has a Unicorn ever existed? Can it be proved they never existed? And will the doctors be able to find out what is wrong with Dad?

Sometimes fate and fantasy have a strange way of interweaving themselves. Dad had been examined by several different doctors and none of them could find out what was causing the pain. Life is a mystery in itself; unpredictable; unreliable; just as you think you've got it all sorted out, something comes a cropper.

"Come on, Jenny!" I held out my hand. "I think we'd better let

Granddad have a rest." I could see Mum was itching to have a word with that kind doctor again.

I kissed Dad's forehead and led Jenny out of the room, taking her down the corridor to the window facing out over the children's play area. Soon I could hear my mother's footsteps coming towards us. I turned to look at her. Her tired, lined face said it all: more tests, more waiting.

The three of us made our way along the corridors towards the play area. While Jenny started up a Unicorn conversation with another little girl sitting on a swing, Mum and I looked on. "Do you think we should tell David to come down?" she whispered. My first reaction was that he should have been told of all of this in the first place. I know he's my kid brother, and I know he's a very busy man with a stressful job, a possessive wife, and four children, two from a previous marriage, to drive him to the point of despair. I felt angry because I always thought David was the special one. He was the eldest son, the cleverest, the best looking. I seemed to be the one left behind to clear up all the mess left by him. I'd even acted as a bridge between him and his ex-wife, in order that he could have regular access to his children.

"Of course he jolly well ought to know!" I burst out, and wished I hadn't, because Jenny looked shocked at me, and Mum looked stunned.

"I'm sorry," I said, and hugged Mum close to me. Ever since Mike had walked out on me, I found it hard not to lash out. And it always seemed to be at those who least deserved it. But life is meant to be a challenge. Only the strongest survive. Sadly the weakest are swept away. Just like the Unicorns. Oh dear…

"Were they stupid?" Jenny's cartoon video had finished. We had enjoyed a hot plate of fish and chips and mushy peas, and maybe my daughter had decided it was time to put childish things aside and get a reality check.

"The Unicorns?" I was struggling to find David's new mobile number. He was always updating it to stop his ex-wife from pestering him. The problem was that as soon as he got a new number, she would ring me and ask me for his new one. It was starting to become a very silly game.

"No," I answered. "The Unicorns weren't stupid. Not really. Just a bit misguided."

"What does misguided mean?"

Again Mum came to the rescue. She knelt down to Jenny's level. "It means they didn't understand how urgent it was for them to jump on to Noah's ark. They thought they had lots of time to play."

"Will Granddad have time to play again?" Jenny bit her lip, waiting for the answer.

"Oh, Jenny!" Mum hugged her tightly and said, "Granddad isn't very well, but I know the doctors will find out what is wrong with him."

"So he will be able to play with me again!" Jenny managed to wriggle out of Mum's arms and ran off to her toy chest. She raced back with a toy horse. "How can I make him into a Unicorn?"

Mum and I looked at each other. "Erm, we could try a piece of plasticine," I suggested.

While we were struggling to achieve this marvellous piece of engineering, the phone rang. I answered it. It was David. His ex-wife had told him I'd sounded very worried when she'd spoken to me the previous day. That I'd mentioned about going to the hospital. "Why ever didn't you tell me?" he said.

"I guess I thought I could fix things from this end," I answered. "Dad's ill. They don't know what's wrong with him. We're waiting to hear."

"I'm on my way now!" said David hurriedly.

I tried to catch him before he ended the call. "Oh, David! You don't happen to know anything about Unicorns, do you?"

As soon as I replaced the receiver, the phone rang again. It was the hospital. They had some news on Dad at last.

I don't remember that drive to the hospital. I can just picture Jenny in a green dress she had been wearing every day for the past five days. She was clutching the little toy horse, desperately trying to keep the plasticine horn attached to it. The rest was a blur of grey and white and glass corridors.

A nurse took Jenny to one side of the room, while the doctor showed us the X-rays.

"It's very, very hard to see. But it's that little thing which has been causing so much pain." At first I couldn't make head nor tail of it. Mum was peering at it, too. And then we saw the little shadow.

"We would like to operate as soon as possible, before he gets too weak," he urged.

Mum nodded slowly. I put my arm around her. Jenny had the nurse in stitches over her plasticine horned toy.

For the next forty-eight hours I worked in a mechanical mode, emptying and refilling the washing machine, scraping plasticine off the kitchen table, and when David arrived with Lindy, I had to find clean towels and sheets. Lindy was the eldest child of his second marriage. She was less than a year older than Jenny. Luckily the two girls hit it off straightaway. It was probably helped by the little present Lindy had for Jenny.

"Why, David. It's exquisite!" I admired the tiny, silver, jewelled Unicorn. "However did you manage it?"

"I may be a bad brother, a terrible father and have no sense of responsibility." He grinned. "But even I have my moments!"

The next morning there was quite a family gathering at the hospital. A very young and very pretty nurse smiled at us and said, "The doctor is ready to see you now."

David squeezed my hand. Mum was ahead of us, ready to hear the news. But before we could stop her, Jenny ran up to the doctor. She beamed and held up the shiny figure. The doctor took it and lifted it up to the light, squinting at the brightness.

"Quite amazing. We operated. It was a complete success. Benign. No further treatment necessary."

Although I had spoken to him before on several occasions, for the first time I noticed how very blue his eyes were. He handed the figure back to Jenny. "And as for you, young lady, I suggest you take this precious object home and keep it in a safe place, so you can show Granddad when he comes to see you."

Soon the doctor had merged with the other white coats at the far end of the corridor.

We were allowed to peek in at Dad, who was still recovering from the effects of the anaesthetic. He would be too tired to see us all today. But we knew there would be tomorrow. Jenny held up the Unicorn, before I whisked her out of the way. She'd had enough attention for one day.

As our family walked back to the car park, David quipped, "Of course Jenny's going to think it was the Unicorn that magicked away her Granddad's pain."

I smiled back at him. "Well, it wouldn't hurt to let her believe that, would it?"

I watched my brother gaze at the two little girls marvelling at the colours in the bright sunshine. He never answered that question.

There was no need.

A LOVE STORY

I think the summer's coming to a close now. Even though I haven't watered my lawn, it's definitely got a greenish tinge to it. It even rained in the night. Heavy, relentless rain. I need to get the hole in the roof fixed before autumn sets in. It can only be a little hole because the roofer I found in the little green book says he can't locate exactly where it is. All I know is that the hole is big enough to allow enough drops of rainwater to pitter-patter on to my collection of bric-a-brac in the attic. I had to struggle up there to shift a few boxes around. I don't mind those ugly old bits of crockery my aunt left me getting damp, but the photos are irreplaceable.

I live at Number Three in a small village with stone walls, one pub, an independently owned grocery store and a little primary school struggling to keep its doors open. I heard that if they couldn't find one more pupil then it would have to close. So thank heaven little Clara has come to live in Number Twelve.

"Hello Mrs Berry."

"Good morning Clara, dear. And what can I do for you today?"

I pretend to be a little strict. You can't let them wrap you round their little finger, can you? And Clara is one of the sweetest natured little girls I have met since my own nieces grew up and flew off to destinations unknown. They send me Christmas cards, but it's not the same as when their dear mother and I struggled to get them back and forth from school, play dates and hospital appointments. Life was so hectic for so many years that we didn't have time to think and take stock. Now I even have time to stop and smell the roses. That's after I have pruned them and treated them for black spot.

Clara is standing on my doorstep. I haven't seen her for three weeks. She and her parents spent that time in a gîte in France. I am sure Clara has grown an inch or two since term ended. Or it might be the green wellies she is wearing have a little heel to them. Never mind all that, I am delighted to see my little friend looking so well and keen to get to work again.

"I'm doing a school project." Clara is waving a yellow clipboard at me. "We have been asked to talk to people about the war."

Here we go, I think. I remember my eldest niece asking me if I was alive when dinosaurs roamed the earth. Although to be fair, she was about two years younger than Clara, and this was before you could Google everything.

I look up the road towards Number Twelve. Her handsome daddy waves at me and shrugs. I know what that means: Indulge her, please. I'll wash my jeep, and mow your lawn when it needs it before the autumn rains. Perhaps he can recommend a better roofer, too.

"Well, Clara. You had better come on in." I put the kettle on. A cup of tea for me. A glass of milk for Clara. A plate of biscuits for us to share.

"I've got a list of questions," says Clara. "Is it okay if I ask you them now?"

"What, all of them?" I tease.

"Yes, please." She smiles. She's lost another baby tooth. I try not to feel sad. I am sure her adult teeth will grow through nice and straight. If they don't, they can fix them with braces now, can't they? Not like when I was a child and we had to clean our teeth with soot after sticking our toothbrushes up the chimney.

I don't tell Clara all about that. She wants to know what I did during the war. World War Two. I think Clara will either be an actress

or a schoolteacher when she grows up. She certainly has the imagina-
tion for the former and the persistence for the latter.

"Were ladies allowed to join the army, Mrs Berry?"

"I think some did, Clara. But I was a bit too young, so I became a
land girl instead and helped on the farms."

"Didn't you get bombed?"

"Only a bit. An enemy plane dropped a bomb in a wood about two
miles from my home. It made a huge crater. It's now a pond." I don't
tell her about the people killed in the café.

"Did you go hungry?"

"No. My parents ran a grocery shop." I don't tell Clara that I used
to sneak downstairs in the middle of the night and help myself to the
broken biscuits.

I feel quite exhausted with all the questions, and decide to let Clara
look through the old photos I have rescued from the leaky attic. I am
going to ask her to wash her hands first so she doesn't get sticky biscuit
fingers all over them. But I can hear her washing them in the little sink
in the cloakroom under the stairs.

I leave her to look through the pictures while I do the washing up.
My mind wanders back to the days when I lived in the rooms above the
grocery store.

I don't hear Clara padding up behind me, and jump when she taps
me on the arm, and shows me a wedding photo. "Is this your wedding,
Mrs Berry?"

The photo is faded, slightly torn and that leaky roof has allowed a
little staining around the edges. The beautiful bride isn't me. I am the
little bridesmaid being held by the lady in the dark suit. The handsome
groom in the RAF uniform was a Spitfire pilot getting married to my
aunt, the grandmother of my nieces. Their mother was my first cousin,

who was more like a sister to me. So that makes them my first cousins once removed.

I decide it's all a little too complicated for the present.

Clara won the class prize for her project, and I was invited to go and see the little exhibition in the school hall. My heart skipped a beat when I saw that the photograph I had lent Clara had been copied and touched up. It looked as good as new. In addition, it had been selected with a few other photos to be put on a digital screen slideshow.

'What a lovely wedding.' I turned to look at the speaker. "Hello," said a young lady who could have passed as a grown-up version of my friend Clara. "I'm Clara's teacher." As my photo slid into view again, she said, "You looked beautiful, Mrs Berry."

I smiled and thanked her, and just before the next slide appeared on the silver screen, I could have sworn the little girl in the photo winked at me!

STAR BRIGHT

For the last year I have watched my brothers and sisters take their turn to leave for the Old Country. Part of me has always envied them in their certainty, and wished that I could take the place of each of them as they have turned their backs on our New World. My arms are empty. Yet another, darker side of me holds within a deep fear, a dread of the time when it will be my turn to go back; a fear of what I may discover upon my return, a fear of not belonging anymore. And yet, return I will, for it is in my destiny, as it is in the destiny of all of us who live here together in harmony.

"Come, little one!" My master holds out his hand. "Come!" He senses my reluctance. "Come! It is your time. You understand what is expected of you?" Even as he takes my hand I know that he expects more of me. For some unknown reason, out of all of my brothers and sisters, he has chosen me. I will journey through the galaxies like a spider spinning her web. My master whispers a message in my ear to be passed on to other chosen ones. I turn to survey my homeland. For this is how I think of it now; as if I have always lived here, always belonged. It is as if I have always meant to be here. Yet my quasar journey has already begun. As I slowly release my grip on his hand, that bright, bright light fades into the glow of a distant planet. A falling sensation fills my being. I actually feel cold shoot through my body like a pointed shaft of ice. I am moving so fast that the air hisses in my ears. I wince with pain. My hair feels as if it is being tugged out in handfuls. That old ache - I remember it now - of rheumatism knifes into the joints of my extremities. Falling, I am falling, down, down, down, ever downwards. Will I miss my appointed destination and drop helplessly into the bowels of Hell?

I dreamt about it once, I remember now. Once when I was still living in the Old Country. I dreamt I was sleepwalking in my grandmother's walled garden. Beyond the wall was the edge of a cliff and a sheer drop into the open sea.

In this dream I jumped over the wall like a mischievous sprite, despite my grandmother's protestations that I should come back into the warmth and safety of her ivy-clad cottage. "The cliff edge! Mind the cliff edge!" I heard her scream. Those were the last words I heard her utter. I was falling, down, down, down, down into the depths of Hell. And slowly I was burning up in the flames of damnation.

Then next I knew my mother was at my bedside, soothing me, telling me to hush now, that it was only a bad dream. While she sat with me, soothing my hot brow, I felt safer than anywhere in the world. Yet as soon as the door clicked shut behind her, even with my little fairy light beside me to chase away the shadow demons, I listened for them. They were out there waiting for me. As my mother's final footfall resonated on the cold hall floor, they were tapping at my window, coercing me to let them in, damn me. I would draw the patchwork quilt over my little golden head and beg them to go away. I wanted to call out to my mother again, for I knew that as soon as they heard her magic footfalls, they would flee screaming like banshees all the way back down to their Hell-hole. But I also knew that should I call out to my mother again, she would be angry at me disturbing her once more from her television programme. Once was acceptable, twice was unbearable. I had tried it before and earned a slap. I was caught between two dangers: that of the banshees and that of the wrath of my frustrated mother. I never did come to terms with the lesser of the two evils. But my mother had endless patience with me once; once when I was little and Daddy was still living with us. She would even sing me to sleep."Starlight, Starbright..."

Every night she would sing to me. Then after he left, when I asked her to sing to me again, she snapped "You're too old for lullabies. Now go to sleep!"

That must have been the moment when I grew up. Starlight...Ah yes, seeing the night sky and all its jewels reminds me of how it was before...Before. What's this? My eyes are stinging now. Tears? I'd almost forgotten how it felt to cry. Now I remember those endless tears I cried when my lover, the only man I had ever really loved, left me for another. It hurts to cry in this cold; for as the salt water seeps from my tear ducts, it is immediately frozen into tiny diamonds. Now I seem to be slowing a little. I have time to taste the planets of the Old Country. I sweep past Pluto and Charon, then on through the dark hydrogen clouds of Neptune, along towards methane-blue Uranus, and loop the ice hoops of my second favourite planet. How breathtakingly beautiful is floating Saturn! My only regret is that I have no one with me to share its delights: its lilac and honey-tinged clouds, with the golden and silver rings reaching up towards a turquoise heaven, glittering with starlight. I have to tear myself away and journey onwards towards deafening Jupiter, carefully dodging the burning red storm. Fiery, rainless Venus fizzes underneath as I fly squint-eyed through its mustard clouds; then on to indigo-skied Mars with its asymmetrical moons, and precious life forms only my master knows the reason for.

As I approach the red planet, the words my master whispered to me a million quasars ago come forth: Your time will come. Soon. Swiftly round the Sun and on, on, on I go, untiring; and yet my form glistens with the moisture of the Universe, frazzles as I skirt the Sun back towards Mercury with its light and dark sides, and on to the silent Moon. There I stand in awesome solitude. If a mortal were to find a road to Earth, it would take him fifteen years to walk from here. So why hasn't he built a road? I shake my head in sadness, resisting the temptation to look back over my shoulder at my multi-quasar quest. I hear my master's voice. "Humility," is all it says.

In the distance I see a glowing marble. As I near it, it becomes bluer and greener. Yet it is so small that I could hold it in the palm of my hand. Though it is tiny, I have to reluctantly admit that I find it achingly beautiful. Its beauty is intensified by a silver gauze that encases it. Then as I move nearer to focus on it, Truth dispels the myth: the precious silver gauze is but a mantle Earth has fashioned for itself. That mantle, my ancient wisdom informs me, is called Pollution. This wisdom also leads me to the one gateway through the heat shield.

Falling, falling, falling. Down, down, down. Thud! What an undignified landing! And it is raining! Ugh! How little the Old Country has changed since I left it. I am in the car park of a superstore. Old people are arguing over some triviality, there are oil patches everywhere, stretched further by the incessant rain. Pieces of broken glass are scattered all around the Bottle Bank, waiting there for little children to pick them up and cut their shell-like palms. A youth is about to smash the side window of a smart blue car. But then the owner was foolish to have left her handbag on the front seat. On the pathway leading up towards the superstore, a middle aged man in a neat grey suit is endeavouring to scrape off the dog excrement he has stepped in.

My tears fall freely now. I taste the bitter salt. I do not know who I am crying for. Part of me is crying for this world I left behind reluctantly in my innocence; part of me weeps for the children on whose shoulders rides the destiny of this world. It is enough. I do not wish to see any more. I do not need to. My ancient wisdom has furnished me with all the answers to satisfy my curiosity. I have business to attend to. There is no time for sentimental journeys. My Knowledge has brought me to a house. It is the smallest dwelling on the narrow street. The front garden is merely a tiny square of unweeded grass. Here little flourishes other than the dandelions. For the first time since my return I feel a smile purse my lips. Dandelions. Real survivors. I remember my mother's single-handed losing battle with them. Our house was very much like this. Perhaps it is the chipped window frames, or the peeling blue paint on the door. A feeling stronger than I have ever felt before runs through my being.

I know this place. I have already been here. I know where he is. He has grown weary waiting for me. Our china blue eyes meet in perfect understanding.

My arms are full again. Then, for a fraction of a second, I feel a stiff reluctance in his frail body. "Who are you? And where are you taking me?"

"I am an Angel. I am taking you Home."

THE DAY SHE CHANGED FOREVER

(a novella)

CHAPTER ONE

Hear No Evil, See No Evil and Speak No Evil

If you see a young man on a motorbike, racing towards the border, please tell somebody. He says his name is Sven, but he is a liar.

My name is Anouska. Today is the day I changed forever.

Before this unfathomable thing happened there was nothing special about being me.

I just was me. Me. It seems strange to think of myself as a sole being now. I have learned so much in the fleeting hours of this day that I feel I am more than one personality. I am a bigger person than I was yesterday.

I lived in a small town that relied on coal and potatoes to keep its community heart beating. My father was a miner and my mother worked part-time in the small, local supermarket. When she was not working, she cared for my little brother, David, and me.

I ache for my family. Part of me imagines that they will find me alive. Another part feels a kind of deadness of being. The alive part has taken the lives of my mother, my father and my little brother and made me the bigger person that I have become.

I know I have to be brave. But every now and then I feel the tears burning my cheeks and it is so very hard not to cry. I cry for my family, my friends, my little town soon to be lost in the chaos. I cry for the little girl that I used to be. It seems so very long ago. So very far away.

It is my little brother David's fifth birthday. Because it is a Sunday we have to go to chapel before my father allows David to open his presents. I think it is a silly rule. I think my mother thinks so, too. But she avoids looking in my eyes as we put on our thick fur bonnets and tie up our sealskin boots, ready to trudge across the fallow field to the little chapel.

"Please, Daddy. Please may I open just one little present?" David's blue eyes look piercingly up at my father.

"No, David. You must wrap up warm. Otherwise you will be too cold to enjoy your presents when you come home. You have to learn patience."

Poor David. I held his little hand as we trekked through the deep snow, following in our father's footsteps. Soon we were joined by other townspeople. Jan, the butcher man, bounded across and laughed and joked with my parents as he told them about a big bull they had to chase around the slaughterhouse ten times before they could kill him.

David laughed. It made me feel sick. I hate it when the marketers come to take away the calves. Their mothers bellow and howl for hours afterwards. Their hot breath steaming up the valley we call home.

I remember this day because it was my brother's birthday. But there is also another darker reason why I remember it. You see because the usual path to the chapel was blocked by snowdrifts, it became easier for us to cut through the pine forest. Usually my father forbade us ever to enter the forest. He said that it was an evil place and we should never go there. But he broke his own rule this day because he knew there was no other choice.

"Keep close to me," he said. "Keep close. Do not wander from the path."

I felt David's hand grip mine more tightly. My mother was happily talking to Jan. She never seemed to be afraid of anything.

There was such a stillness in the forest. Heavy snow casts a stillness on a landscape anyway. Before the snow comes, we feel it in the air. Many of the townspeople complain of headaches. But when the snow falls they feel a lightness of being. It is as if something magical has been released into the air, and down come the patterned crystals of snow.

I hated the feeling I had in the forest. I hated it even more than Jan's talk of shooting the bull right between the eyes. I hated it more than the way he smoked that arrogant cigar.

But the hate feeling I had for the forest was a different hate feeling. It was a pulling feeling. It was as if it were challenging me to face up to it.

My father was right. The forest was bad. Terrible things had happened here. I wanted to hurry through and get to the chapel. My feet were already starting to ice up, and David's grasp was making my fingers tingle.

"Daddy!" David shouted. "There's a pond over there. It's all frozen. Can I skate on it when we come back from chapel?"

"What?" My father laughed. "And who will open your presents?" He turned and lunged forwards to sweep up little David and swing him round. They reminded me of snow angels on a carousel.

My father plonked him down and then pretended to whisper to me: "Don't tell him that the Pine Goblin lives under the ice of that pond. For if you do, he won't sleep for a week." He winked at me and I winked back. David tried to copy us, but only succeeded in blinking.

It was such a happy family moment. But I sensed the fear coming from that frozen pond. At David's age it would have been enough for me to stay away from the dreaded Pine Goblin. I would have snuggled up under my duvet, secure in the knowledge that he couldn't possibly find his way to our cottage. Provided no older person fed me with scary stories, I would fall asleep upon thinking what outfit I would save up for my Barbie doll with my pocket money.

There were strange stories about the Pine Goblin. My friend, Peter, told me the Pine Goblin ate kittens and found his way to people's homes by following their footsteps in the snow. Jimmy Knott, the school crazy boy, said the Pine Goblin had eaten one of his mother's babies. That earned him a detention. It was very funny at the time.

My father had warned us to stay away from the forest. To stay away especially after dark. I was a big sister. Old enough to be curious. Young enough to be foolish. I knew that I would persuade Peter, Jimmy Knott, and his twin sister, Alicia, to sneak out after dark and go and check out if there really was a stupid fat goblin in that pond.

Another very good reason for reckoning with the Pine Goblin was that our black cat, Malisha, had gone missing.

CHAPTER TWO

Witch's Cat

Malisha was a witch's cat. We knew that because we found her on Hallowe'en. A tiny black kitten, with amber eyes, squeezed itself into our tool shed, and of course into our hearts on the day we scooped out pumpkins and counted the days till Candlemas.

"She's my cat," whined my brother, scooping up the shaking kitten and clasping her to his big, woolly, red jumper. "I saw her first."

"You must share her," corrected my mother. "Shall we call her Malisha after the witch's assistant in that book your Aunt Talia wrote?"

Craftily my mother had made Malisha her own. But then she was the one who fed her milk rusks and tender pieces of cod. It was always my mother who came home first to find Malisha curled up asleep on the blue mat in front of the hearth.

It was just over a year ago Malisha had chosen us. Today she had left.

Or did the Pine Goblin take her?

David was exhausted over his presents and went to bed an hour earlier than his normal eight o'clock. This gave me chance to slip out and knock for Peter, Jimmy and Alicia.

Peter's parents had been killed in a road accident when he was four years old, so he lived with his grandmother in the cottage nearest the strange forest. His grandmother had been poorly. She had not attended chapel and Peter had stayed home to look after her.

I tapped gently on the little front window. I knew the grandmother would be asleep in the back room. Probably snoring with her mouth open. Peter would be reading by the hearth. He read so many books and wanted to be an engineer when he was old enough to leave the town.

He came to the door.

"Hi!" he whispered. "How's the birthday boy?"

"Asleep." I smiled. "Do you want to knock for Jimmy and Alicia?" He looked deep into my eyes. "Do we have to ask them to tag along?"

I looked down at my boots. I knew I was blushing. "Yes. We need help to find Malisha."

"Stupid moggy wandered off again?" Peter turned to tug down his thick, brown overcoat. "Perhaps she has a boyfriend."

"She's only a kitten still," I snapped.

I could hear him pulling on his boots. He then said, "But some cats grow up quicker than others. And yes, maybe we should invite Alicia and Jimmy along."

I tried to ignore a feeling of jealousy as he mentioned Alicia's name before Jimmy's. None of us were little kids anymore. It was a small town and it was too easy to grow too fond of each other.

I ran over to the Knott's cottage. It was the biggest cottage in our lane and the oldest. Some folks said it was haunted. But I thought even a poltergeist couldn't bear to share a home with Jimmy. He was okay in a gang and in small doses. But it was scary to think that somebody would marry him one day.

Alicia must have seen us approach. She opened the door before I needed to knock.

"Hello Anouska." I saw her peer over my shoulder to look at Peter. Everybody in class knew she was sweet on him. I felt sorry for her.

She had all the trademarks of beauty: blonde hair, blue eyes, a slim figure. But there was something lacking in her. Maybe it was because she was always coming down with viruses and it depleted her strength.

"Hi Alicia." I grinned. "Wrap up warm. We are going to find the cat that left without leaving a note."

She was still looking at Peter. "Can't we just play tag or something? Surely the cat will come back home when it's hungry." She twisted a strand of hair sulkily. I felt like slapping her one. We were much too old to play tag. What she wanted was to trick Peter into kissing her.

I was worried if he did that he would catch something. Lately I'd been feeling very confused about things. About my life. About my body. About what I wanted to do when I left school. It seemed all three of us had one day been snotty little kids. Now we were old enough to have a few choices. But we didn't know how to use them.

We were only eleven. But we were on the edge of something.

Suddenly Alicia plunged towards me. Her stupid brother had shoved her.

"Come on, sissy! Get yer clobber on. We are going to party."

Jimmy had arrived. I no longer wanted to slap his sister, I wanted to punch him right in his silly, slobbering mouth.

When Peter looked at me, I felt a tug of thrill deep in my stomach. When Jimmy looked at me, I wanted to vomit.

"My father says we should never go through the forest alone." I stood in the middle of them. "And why weren't you two at chapel today?"

Jimmy and Alicia looked at each other with a secret knowledge. I hated this Twins Conspiracy they shared and tried to break it when I could.

Jimmy looked down at his own big boots.

So Alicia tried to tell me: "My mother had to go and visit a sick aunt. Our father overslept."

So he was still drinking.

"Will he mind you going into the strange forest?"

"Anouska! What's with this strange forest stuff?" And with that Jimmy picked up a huge ball of snow and stuffed it down the back of my coat.

But I knew he was just as frightened of going in there as the rest of us.

Especially now it was after dark.

CHAPTER THREE

The Frozen Pond

Peter was the biggest in our group. So we let him stomp his way through the first winter's snow towards the opening in the forest.

"My Dad'll kill me and Alicia when he finds out what we're doing." Jimmy threw in one of his ambiguous remarks. Five minutes of his company and I was already weary of him. I wanted to comment that his dad was likely too drunk to care. It's funny how insightful I was even then. Had I been less so, then perhaps I would have found Jimmy less irritating. Alicia had her Twin Thing to inoculate her. Whereas Peter was usually thinking about something scientific and let Jimmy's sarcasm go right over his head.

I guess I was the one left to chew on this little bone.

Moreover I wanted to find my Malisha.

After five more minutes walking in the deep snow, Alicia was starting to struggle to keep up. Part of me was delighted, because it meant she couldn't keep stalking Peter. But the kinder side of my nature told me to take her hand and help her through. Let's face it, we girls have enough to do competing with the boys. We really shouldn't fight between each other.

Her hand felt skinny and light in mine, despite the added layers of our individual glove-wear.

I'm too young to be nostalgic. But I do remember thinking back to when we were very little and starting infant school. That day we held hands when we went into the classroom for the first time. Alicia said

Jimmy always crushed her bones together and it was enough just having him as her protector. Had Jimmy been a nicer boy then I think I would have been jealous of that. Sometimes I used to pretend Peter and I were twins. There was only a day between us in age. So if we'd had a mother with a long labour then it would have been feasible.

"Come on, you weedy little women!" Jimmy turned to holler back. Peter was already out of sight.

He must have reached the pond by now. The frozen pond.

Where the Pine Goblin lived.

What a ridiculous story. Who believed in that kind of rubbish at our age?

I decided to annoy Jimmy:

"How many babies did the Pine Goblin eat?"

He chose to ignore me and turned to continue. The only sound was the crunching in the snow and Alicia's laboured breathing.

I wondered if she and I should turn back. With her mother away, it was doubtful her father would know what to do if she got ill. Now I realised I needed her, I didn't want to lose her. For who else would protect me from her brother's forced insanity? Also, I decided she wouldn't have enough breath to snog Peter.

"Can we stop a minute, Anouska?"

I turned to look into her face. Her lips were almost blue. I called to the others, but there was no response.

"Shall I take you back, Alicia?" I willed her to make a miraculous recovery. It wasn't just I wanted my cat back now, I wanted to catch up with Peter. This place was spooking the living night lights out of me.

Alicia must have read my thoughts. "Let's find Malisha," she said.

The boys must be far ahead now. At this point the trees thickened and our cries would have been absorbed into their bark.

Suddenly there was a cry like a wolf.

I saw Alicia jump and the look of horror passed her face, turning it from blue to grey to pink. It was an amazing thing.

Then she burst into tears. "I want my mummy," she sobbed. "I don't know when she's coming home. Daddy's so horrid to her when he's been drinking."

I put my arm around her. "Don't worry. It's only a wild dog calling for its pups." It was hard getting close to her because our coats were so thick. "Has your dad not been able to find work much?"

Her father had wanted to start his own cab business. He loved cars and driving. But very few people in our little town could afford a taxi. Most people walked to their destinations, or caught the twice-weekly bus into the bigger towns beyond the valley.

My mother had said Jan told her that Alicia's dad had been a bus driver once, but that he had been sacked for drunk-driving. If this were true then it was a very good reason for why he was unemployed. Further south in our country people are imprisoned for driving when under the influence of alcohol. It was no wonder their mother kept going away to have breaks from him.

The wild dog cried out again.

I had lied to Alicia, of course. That was no more a wild dog than I am Empress of India.

Suddenly I heard running feet coming back towards us. Jimmy appeared with the look of the hunted on his face. "Run! Run! You stupid women!" He grabbed us both by our collars to will us to get out of there.

Peter appeared in pursuit, and we hotfooted like floundering abominable snowmen back to the entrance of the forest.

When we had all recovered from the exertion, I framed a question: "What the hell was all that about?"

Peter and Jimmy exchanged eye contact.

Peter said, "Look, girls, Anouska's dad's right. There is something vile about that pond. Something obviously happened there once. Maybe a long time ago. We shouldn't mess with something we don't understand."

Alicia said, "Peter's got a point there, Anouska. I'm so sorry about your cat." She squeezed my hand before turning to follow Jimmy back to their cottage.

"Do you want me to walk you back?" Peter asked.

"No thanks." I was blinking back the tears as I trudged off home.

"See you at school tomorrow." His voice was absorbed into the ice of the night.

We can all have our secrets, I thought bitterly.

CHAPTER FOUR

The Funny Tricks of Time

Although more terrible things have happened to me, I will always remember that night. That icy, bone-chilling night I trudged home, the tears stinging my young face. I felt suspended between Peter's treachery and the certainty of my father's anger at flouting his instruction.

I stopped and listened. I counted my breaths as I awaited the inevitable. And the inevitable came.

"Bang!" The sky burst open and released its heavenly crystals.

That night the depth increased to ten inches. By the time I softly unlatched the door, my footsteps were hidden by the whiteness.

I had nothing to fear. My parents were more concerned with David. He had awoken, screaming feverishly. My mother was mopping his brow with a cold flannel and my father was trying to get through to the doctor. But the lines were down.

"Anouska! Run to Doctor Hillman's house." He seemed to overlook the fact I was already dressed for a snow outing. "Quickly! David needs some penicillin."

I turned and launched myself back out the door, down the path and towards the Hillman's house. Theirs was the farthest house from the strange forest. Possibly the safest place to live.

But my journey was wasted. The doctor had already been called out to an emergency. His wife told me he had gone to visit Alicia, who'd collapsed after being out in the snow. Her father feared she had pneumonia.

I stood and stared as her lips moved, framing those words.

But it couldn't be. It couldn't have happened so quickly. I also wondered how it was that the telephone lines had gone down. I must have looked frozen because she insisted I came in and drank a hot chocolate with her by the hearth.

Mrs Hillman was a lot older than my mother, and I think quite a lot older than her husband. My mother said she thought Mrs Hillman was from another country, and had been brought to this country as a child because the family were not happy in their own homeland. She said that this had happened to many people during and after the Second World War. Sometimes whole small towns and villages had disappeared and those who were left had to find a new country to call their own.

It sounded very sad to me. I couldn't imagine how I would react if that happened to me. At the time my mother told me about Mrs Hillman, I never thought it ever would.

The Hillman's house was a lot bigger than ours because they needed the extra room for the patients' waiting area and the surgery. I had never been in the back parlour before and I was amazed at how old fashioned it was. It was like stepping back into a time before even my grandmother was born. The colours were dark, the curtains heavy, and there was a very old grandfather clock ticking away in the corner furthest away from the hearth.

That was when I was petrified. I looked at the hands on the clock. It was five minutes to midnight! But that meant I had been out for almost four hours! As I warmed my hands on the hot chocolate mug, I tried to work out how the time had moved so swiftly. I was sure that I had only been out with the other kids for about an hour. Maybe two at tops. So where had the time flown?

Had I wandered mysteriously into the strange forest and somehow walked full circle? Or was I going snow crazy? My aunt told me about that once. She said it happened to the great Polar explorers when they risked their lives to be the first to reach the Poles. The intense cold did something to their senses and they became literally frozen in time. They would leave the relative warmth and safety of their tents to walk outside for a little while. But sometimes they would never return. Their colleagues would find them frozen only yards from the tent. On occasions their bodies would never be found.

Mrs Hillman placed her palm on my forehead.

"My dear," she said kindly. "I do believe you are running a fever, too. There must be a virus doing its rounds. I think we shall have to advise the schoolmaster to close the school for a week to let this thing pass through."

She made it sound as if it were a living thing. A thing.

A thing like the Pine Goblin.

I wondered if we had all been cursed.

We never found Malisha. But the virus went away after a fortnight. We all returned to school a little older and I think a little wiser.

Something had changed between Peter, Alicia, Jimmy and me. We no longer waited for each other before and after school. At playtime we tended to hang out with the other kids. I never found out what Peter and Jimmy saw that night and why it had frightened them so much

But there was more to it than that. We were growing up and away from each other. It was good to socialise with the other kids. In less than a year we would all be going our separate ways to different schools, so it was better that we didn't get too fond of one another.

Of course I was too young to think this way at the time. Although I had a feeling of fate and acceptance at the way of things, I didn't understand why I felt sad sometimes; and at other times I needed to be surrounded by lots of people and loud music to drown out the silence.

My parents didn't like me hanging round the coffee bar that had recently opened opposite Jan's butcher shop. They said it wouldn't be long before the bikers discovered it. Then the street fights would start. So my father bought me a little record player, so I could play my pop records in my bedroom. I would stay in there for hours, when I'd finished my homework, drowning myself in the magic of the music, and dreaming one day of being famous.

By now Peter was attending a private boarding school. His grandmother had to go into a home to be looked after. Jimmy and Alicia were being tutored by a retired schoolteacher who travelled by bicycle three times a week to impatiently set them impossible maths questions.

I was one of three pupils to gain a place at the girls' grammar school in the next valley. I had to walk there and back six times a week. It was a full schedule and left me very little time to seek out my old school friends.

CHAPTER FIVE

Feeling Guilty

I should have tried harder. I realise that now more than ever. What Peter, Alicia, Jimmy and I had had wasn't perfect. But it had been special. People who knew you as a child remember a part of you that was magical.

I used a heavier homework-load and a longer school day as an excuse to distance myself from my old friends. It wasn't even enough that David was a daily reminder of my old school. They could even wear sweatshirts now. I felt envious of David's bright red and white one. It looked much cooler than my drab navy pleated skirt and heavy blazer.

One day in the middle of June I knew I had to wake myself up. I'd been spending far too much time mulling over my algebra sums and essays. It was midsummer, I was writing my thoughts in my diary, when I realised I'd still not kissed a boy:

Heck! I can't believe I just thought that! Why should it matter anyway? Why should it matter that all the girls in my class have kissed somebody and I haven't. Maybe I should have lied and said I had. Peter was almost a boyfriend. Indeed he might have become my boy-friend if I hadn't gone and stomped off that night we tried to find Malisha.

I guess it was my fault. Perhaps If I'd wanted a boyfriend more, then I would have one. It would just happen. I think Jimmy would go out with me. But I'm not that desperate. Also, I think Jimmy would tease me because I don't wear a bra yet. I wonder if Alicia does. Well, there's only one way to find out. I'll make some excuse to call on them.

I dotted the final full stop, slammed the book shut, and ran down the stairs two at a time.

"I'm off to see Alicia!" I yelled to my mother. She was peeling tatties in the kitchen.

"Say hi to them from me!" she called back, and then I heard her turn the tap full-on.

The Knotts had a gorgeous display of brightly-coloured flowers in their front border. If I'd not been visiting, I might have been tempted to pick some.

Their father answered the door when I rang.

"Hello stranger." He smiled kindly. But I could smell the pub on him. "They're practising their algebra. But you can go on in."

The pretty garden was deceptive. The house was cluttered with cooking smells, dirty shoes, and a pile of newspapers. There was no sign of their mother anywhere.

I trotted into the back parlour where Alicia and Jimmy were sitting at a table covered in books and coloured pencils.

Neither looked up straightaway. When Jimmy did, he said, "Oh, it's you. Nice of you to bother. While you're here, you might as well give us a hand with our sums. A clever little grammar schoolgirl like you must know all the answers."

Alicia looked up and almost managed a smile.

This was the first time I'd seen them closer than a wave across the road for nearly six months. Jimmy was getting even more cynical. Alicia, worryingly more frail. Despite that, she was definitely wearing a bra.

I wanted to walk out. I felt I'd failed on both points. A smart girl with no breasts didn't fit in this part of town. Most of the people who stayed round here married young and completed their families before they were thirty.

I was right to have stayed away. But I was also right to come and lay my ghosts to rest. Alicia and I were friends once. Nothing can change that. But her body was developing faster than her mind and she and I didn't have anything in common anymore.

Of course I still had unfinished business with Jimmy.

I said, "I think you owe me an explanation for what happened that night in the strange forest?"

He didn't rush to answer. But when he did, he said, "And what night might that have been?" He was already getting bum fluff on his top lip. I tried not to imagine how revolting it would feel to kiss him. Yes, it was definitely more sensible to lie about kissing a boy. I would rather dream about kissing one of the popstars on my bedroom wall.

"It doesn't matter," I answered. "We were all trying to frighten each other." I waited for either to answer. But both carried on copying letters and numbers from their textbooks. Looking over Alicia's pink-pullovered shoulder, I realised they were doing work I'd covered in the first week of term at Grammar. "Do you want any help?" I offered.

Jimmy looked up slowly and said, "Oh go back to your posh friends, girlie."

Neither said anything more to me.

I felt the annoying prick of tears behind my eyes. I made excuses for their unkindness. It was because their mother had left them. I guess it could even have been the night we'd searched in vain for Malisha. Because of that they had been forced to grow up more quickly. They saw me as a privileged, spoilt brat, who'd rather study and dream of better things than hang out with a pair of losers.

They were right. But at the time I was too innocent to see it that way. I wanted to be able to find the end of the thread we'd shared as children. I wanted to borrow a little bit of that something we'd shared once when we were little. But I also knew our goodbyes had been said a long time ago. It's just that sometimes it is so very hard to put the bolt on the door of something, without ever being tempted to pull it back occasionally to check nothing's changed.

I ran back to my room and burst into tears on my bed. I didn't even know what I was crying for.

After a few minutes, my mother called up and asked me to wash my hands and come downstairs to set the table for tea.

When I appeared in the kitchen, she pretended not to notice I'd been crying. All she said as I pulled open the cutlery drawer was: "They do so miss their mother."

As June turned into the summer holidays I would sometimes hang around within sight of their house. The flowers grew even more beautiful. I wondered if they'd like to go for a picnic in the valley. As the days grew hotter, my enthusiasm dried out. But there did remain one more thing for me to do before I waved goodbye to my childhood.

CHAPTER SIX

A Disgrace

I knew what I had to do. Something kept going through my mind. It was what my mother had said when I'd returned from the Knott's and burst into tears. She'd said Mrs Knott was a disgrace to her family and the community.

I was too hungry and too upset at the way Jimmy and Alicia had behaved towards me to really care about Mrs Knott's position in the pecking order of the little town. Okay, so she wasn't exactly in the Top Ten Favourite Inhabitants. But how could my mother justify making such a judgemental comment? She hadn't smelt the alcohol and tobacco on Mr Knott's breath. I didn't blame Mrs Knott for running away. I often wanted to do that myself. Jimmy was an obnoxious creep anybody would find hard to love. I couldn't even remember him ever saying a kind word about anybody. Alicia was nicer, but she was so easily influenced by her twin. They were a twin-set and didn't need anybody else in their lives. Surely Mrs Knott realised that before she packed a bag and left them.

I was also starting to get bored of going to chapel each Sunday. Because I had to go to school on Saturdays during the term-time, it meant I had no free days to myself. I was also beginning to wonder if I believed in all the religious stuff being pumped into me. Another thing that bothered me was when people like Jan went to chapel and they still did unchristian things like over-charge people for gristly pieces of meat, passing off mutton for lamb, and I'm sure I heard my mother whisper to the doctor's wife that Jan had two girlfriends.

Another thing I couldn't stand was the way Christians were so judgemental of people. I wasn't ready to challenge my mother on this.

I knew when I did that she would be very angry. But one day I would say something.

Now I was about to do something that would anger my father if he found out. I was about to enter the strange forest and put paid to that nonsense once and for all.

I decided to get up early. The weather was at its hottest and I knew if I made an early start then I would be able to get away before David got up. I didn't want him following me and getting in the way. I knew he wouldn't be able to keep it a secret. So I promised him I'd take him swimming in the lake before the sun got too hot.

I managed to sneak out of the house at six-thirty. It was going to be another beautiful day. Everywhere was quiet. Even the birds seemed to be getting up late this morning. I walked past the Knott's garden, Peter's old home, and towards the entry to the forest. It was noticeably cooler as I dashed between the pines. The ground was dusty beneath my feet and I felt my sandals crushing the ancient pine needles.

I followed the path round towards the pond, and that was when I realised why my father had warned me to stay away:

The pond had all but dried up. There was a ragged rock in its centre, covered in green slime. A lizard scuttled off it as I approached. But the really horrible bit was that embedded in the thick exposed bottom of the pond were chips of bone. Others were sticking out like calcified bulrushes. Then a bubble blew up from underneath and as it burst, a hideous flying thing launched itself out of the dampness and flew off further into the forest.

I wanted to scream. But the sound froze in my throat. I've seen terrible things since that time, but this was the ghastliest image I'd ever seen up to that point. I knew the bones were human remains. They were so broken up and brittle that it must have been decided to leave them there. I knew from what my mother spoke of the War that many atrocities had occurred. People had just been taken from their homes, killed, their bodies burnt and what was left was buried. So many families had been wiped out that there was nobody left to mourn or try to identify the remains.

A morbid part of me was curious enough to make me want to move closer and examine these more carefully. If I cared enough, then maybe in years to come I could return as an adult with people who understood these things and we could collect them in the proper way, to be analysed, labelled and put to rest.

For now I would leave them there. When the autumn rains came they would be covered again by the stagnant waters. Another winter would come and go. At least I knew what all the upset was about.

I needed to return home to have my breakfast and take my little brother swimming in the lake.

The lake is really only a large pond that has the benefit of a secret underground stream to keep it fresh. Every so often a man from the Health Service comes to take a sample of the water to send to a laboratory in one of the bigger cities. My mother says it's because after the War some children contracted polio after swimming in the lake. Of course nowadays we are given a lump of sugar with the vaccine to prevent us from catching it. But the Health Service still likes to keep a check on these things.

David was not a happy boy today. My father had promised to take him down the mine with him, but had changed his mind for some reason. He knew there would be a lot of people worried about the rumoured closure of the mine. I had overheard him telling Jan he didn't want to trouble my mother until the final decision was announced. As it turns out, my father's job remained until the day our lives changed forever.

I tried to coax David into putting on some sun cream. But he refused. Unlike me, he doesn't tan well, and I knew he would burn, despite it being almost the end of summer. His skin is just so sensitive. I knew he would burn and then I would get into trouble with my mother because she had read somewhere that if a child got burnt three times badly, then he stood a very strong chance of getting skin cancer.David had already burnt badly twice. Today would be the third time, and it would be all my fault because I was supposed to be looking after him.

But amazingly he didn't burn. Instead he screamed at me to take him home after half an hour. He wanted to play with his toys indoors. So I took him home.

Because I had got up so early it seemed to be such a long day ahead. My mother was doing some decorating and I was bored now. So again I decided to do something my parents would not approve of. I would visit the new coffee bar opposite Jan's.

And that's where I met my first boyfriend.

CHAPTER SEVEN

As Fate Would Have It

Had my mother not been so busy painting her bedroom a cooler shade of blue, and had my brother not been in such a foul mood, then I would never have met Sven.

The stupid thing is that I really wanted to go to the library. But it was a Wednesday and for some reason a lot of local traders, including the library, decided to shut up shop on a Wednesday. I know that Jan took out Wednesdays to visit the market in one of the bigger cities to replenish his meat supplies. The supermarket, where my mother worked part-time, would await the arrival of the various delivery vans. I wonder if the short-tempered librarian just took time out to read her books instead of banging them with her smudgy date-stamp, or ticking-off anybody smaller than herself returning a book overdue.

Until the coffee bar opened, Wednesdays were a chore. It was often on Wednesdays that children got themselves hurt or into trouble. It was a stupid day anyway. A nothing sort of day. Had it not been a Wednesday, I would have bought myself another tacky teenage magazine and mulled over the problem page, while applying the cheap, sticky lip- gloss attached as a free gift to attract the hesitant buyer. However careful I was, I would always tear the cover when removing the freebie. Sometimes the freebie would have been removed by a sneak-thief. By somebody who was a disgrace to the community. The only thing I'd ever stolen was a beautiful blue bead from the school sewing box. I remember coveting it for several days before awaiting my chance when nobody was looking, and sneaking it into my skirt pocket. I was only four years old and it felt dangerous, yet exciting. The funny thing was that I left it in my pocket till my mother found it. She pulled it out and popped it on to my dressing table, tutting at me.

"It fell in there," I pleaded.

But one bead wasn't enough. I discovered there was another even more beautiful bead in the box. So I took that one, too.

Again, I snuck it into my skirt pocket for my mother to find.

This time she got rattled and said, "Why are you doing this? Don't take any more. Okay?"

I remember this sudden panic of guilt. What if the teacher searched through the box? What if somebody had seen me steal the beads, didn't want me to know, but had told everybody else in the class that I was a thief?

"Should I put them back?" I asked my mother.

"No. Somebody might see you put them back and that could cause even more fuss. Just leave them be. But don't take any more!"

She left it at that and went back downstairs, leaving me to mull over the error of my ways. I felt I should return them. Suddenly the idea of stolen property revolted me. They looked ugly to me now. How stupid it would be to get into trouble over a couple of beads. I stared at their shininess on my dressing table. With one swoop, I swiped them both into my tinny little waste-bin and covered them with some tissues from the box in my parents' bedroom.

At school the next day I sat quietly, watching to see if anybody missed those beads. Surely they must have. But nobody said anything.

When my bin was emptied into the dustbin and put out for the refuse collectors to take away, I wondered if I should sneak out and rummage through for them. I had time to rescue them. After all, I had wanted those beads so badly.

But I let the dustcart transport the beads away, and after time I forgot about being found out. There were other children they would suspect before me.

People like Jimmy.

I entered the coffee bar and a tall, fair-haired boy was waiting for the waitress to mix him a mocha. I hadn't got the taste for coffee yet. So I counted out the money for a chocolate milkshake. I watched him pay for his drink and thank the waitress. He sat at the table nearest the door. A cooling breeze wafted through. All the other tables were taken. His table was the only one with a spare couple of chairs.

So I guess I had to sit opposite him.

Thank heaven I'd brought a week-old magazine with me. It was a stupid tacky teenage one, but without the torn cover. I tried to concentrate on a boring article about a boring band who were trying to make it in the charts with a boring song that sounded like a boring version of another better band's hit record.

"Why do you girls read that rubbish?"

I looked up into a pair of big brown eyes. Most of the people round here were blonde and blue-eyed. I rather liked the combination of fair hair with brown eyes. It made him seem more exotic.

I knew I was blushing. But he was too good looking to pass up.

"It's because the library's closed," I said. "I'd much rather read a proper book."

He smiled in amusement. I liked his perfect white teeth. I liked his mouth. I wanted to kiss him very much indeed.

I could feel myself blushing more deeply. I was desperate to think of something to say. But my brain had disconnected from my mouth, and I just stared at him like a frightened rabbit.

"I'm Sven," he said. "I've moved into the house near the forest." His head wobbled a little, and the way he turned to look out the window and then back towards me reminded me of an actor I couldn't quite pin down.

"Anouska," I said. "My friend Peter used to live there with his grandmother."

"Was he your boyfriend?" Sven dug around in his jacket pocket for a packet of cigarettes. I watched as he pulled one out, put it between his lips and lit it swiftly with a match. He seemed to affect all the movements so efficiently. I had never met anybody like him before.

"Yes," I lied. "We broke up when he went to boarding school."

"So you're in between boyfriends at the moment?" He puffed out a plume of smoke, looked down at his mocha and then up and deep into my eyes.

Heck, I thought. I think he's going to ask me out. But I don't think I'm ready for a proper boyfriend yet. It was like two wiser people were having a discussion in my head. But my stomach was dancing with itself and somehow in the last thirty seconds I'd forgotten how to breathe automatically.

"Do you fancy going to the flicks?" Again, he looked away, looked down, turned and looked back up deep into my eyes. How could he smile at me in that way if he did not think we could fall in love?

James Dean's evil twin.

Didn't he know the cinema shut on Wednesdays?

A very boring, but very sensible part of me realised he was playing games with me. He must have been about nineteen. He could have the pick of the town's schoolgirls. On the other hand, it wouldn't hurt to be friendly. If he was a new kid in town, then he needed to find his feet. There was another fortnight left of the summer holidays. What harm would there be in being friends?

I just wished I hadn't fibbed about Peter being a boyfriend. When Sven stood up, I noticed his biker jacket slip back to reveal the mesh vest that scarcely covered the tattoos on his deep-tanned upper chest: a curious black cat and a goblin's face peering through pine trees.

If you see a young man on a motorbike, racing towards the border, please tell somebody. He says his name is Sven, but he is a liar.

My name is Anouska. Today is the day I changed forever.

Before this unfathomable thing happened there was nothing special about being me. Now I live in the strange forest. Forever lost. Yet here I am, waiting for you to come and find me.